FIRST DOG

AUTHORED BY
LINDA KAY BEGLEY

COVER DESIGN OR ARTWORK BY
DENNIS WACHA

DRAWINGS BY
LINDA KAY BEGLEY

ISBN-10: 1478151927
EAN-13: 9781478151920

Library of Congress Control Number: 2012913997
CreateSpace, North Charleston, SC

DEDICATION

If I could sing like the Shirelles in the early '60s, I would be belting out the lyrics of the song entitled "Dedicated to the One I Love." Dennis Wacha is my best friend; he has always stood by me, helping to make all of my dreams become a reality. My wish for everyone in the world is that you do, or someday you will, have a friend like Dennis.

"This is dedicated to the one I love."

Linda

INTRODUCTION OF
MAIN CHARACTERS

The following four pages are drawings created by the Author to provide the reader with a visual of the main characters; Scout, Snubby, Scholar and Pixie that you will be reading about in this delightful story.

SCOUT

SNUBBY

SCHOLAR

PIXI

CHAPTER 1

It was that magical time of the year again at the Fort Totten Trash Transfer Station in Washington, DC, a place where the garbage from the local residents and businesses was dropped off. In late December, the holiday garbage was a real treat for three doggies, Scout, Snubby, and Scholar, strays who for the past six years had made this their home.

Each of them had his own special place in the pack. Scout was a perky, happy-go-lucky Springer spaniel, who ventured out ahead of the others to explore and made sure the coast was clear. Snubby, a temperamental English bull dog, with wrinkles and lip flaps, was the gruff protector of the group, and Scholar, a multi-breed mutt, was the intellect. They loved the home they'd made for themselves and their motto was: one human's garbage is another dog's treasure.

Scout was at his lookout point, pacing back and forth, waiting eagerly for a garbage truck to arrive — not any truck but the one that picked up the trash on the Pennsylvania Avenue route. He knew all of the routes and the times the garbage would be delivered for each of them. He also knew that the one and only president of the United States lived on

1

Pennsylvania Avenue, and the first family's delectable holiday treats would be delivered at any moment now.

Suddenly, with a jump and wagging of his tail, Scout ran back to camp as fast as he could, shouting, "Yippee! Yippee! Yay! Here it comes, right on schedule...get ready for our White House Christmas."

Snubby looked up and growled, "It's called a White Christmas."

Scout snipped back, "I'm not talking about the snow fall, grumpy. It's our Sugar Plum Fairy Express." And, sure enough, there it was: the good old Fort Totten garbage truck, full of the first family's holiday leftovers.

Snubby groaned, "It's too early to get holiday leftovers. The holiday has just begun."

Scholar spoke up, "Scout is right. It says right here in the *Washington Post* that the first family left town yesterday morning to spend the remainder of their holiday in Hawaii."

Scout shouted, "Come on, gang, let's go," his legs moving as fast as they could go.

Snubby turned to Scholar with a smirk on his face and said, "Well, Mr. Know-It-All, no wonder your owners were upset with your potty habits. You were too busy reading the paper instead of using it to be house-broken."

Scholar knew how to handle Snubby's grumpy comments. So, in his own intellectual way, he looked up and said, "Who would want to go to the bathroom on a perfectly good newspaper?"

Scout, in the meantime, had flung himself right into the middle of the huge heap of freshly dumped garbage.

"Ouch," he howled as he spit out a black and white object. "What is this?"

Scholar ran over to examine the object and said, "Why, it's a Bo ornament."

"What's a Bo ornament?" whined Scout.

Scholar explained, "Bo is the dog of the first family, which makes him the first dog. This year they had a big party, with children making Christmas tree ornaments that looked like Bo out of licorice. A lot of the kids took them home as souvenirs and some of the kids ate them. I guess you got a hold of one that was left over."

In a disenchanted tone, Scout said, "'Left over' is not the word for it. Are you sure it was this Christmas they made'em? This thing is as hard as a rock."

Scholar said, "Come on, let's enjoy our feast. I'll tell you more about Bo later. Look at the bright side: you now have a White House souvenir." Scout carefully buried his Bo ornament and then joined the gang for their holiday feast.

Later that evening, with their bellies full, they talked about how this must be the best place in the world to live, that is if you happen to be a homeless doggie.

Scout said, "Yep, now I know where the saying 'lucky dog' came from. Scholar, can you tell me more about Bo?"

At this, Snubby yawned and said, "Here we go again," plopping his head down.

Scholar began his story, "Well, Bo is a Portuguese water dog. He moved into the White House on April 14, 2009. His official name is 'Amigo's New Hope' but the first daughters, Malia and Sasha, nicknamed him Bo."

With a confused look on his face, Scout asked, "How do you get Bo out of that big, long name?"

Scholar loved having all the answers, so in a very proud voice he said, "He got the name because Malia and Sasha have a cousin with a cat named Bo and their grandfather was nicknamed Diddley."

Scout, now howling with laughter, shouted, "Stop!" and gasped, "What in the diddley squat does the name Diddley have to do with the name Bo?" He continued to roll around laughing, complaining that he ate so much that his laughing was hurting his stomach.

In Scholar's own patient way, he continued with the story: "Michelle's father was nicknamed Diddley, after Bo Diddley, who was a famous American rhythm and blues singer, songwriter, and guitarist. Bo Diddley did a lot for the music industry; he passed away in June 2008."

With wide eyes, Scout said, "Wow! A first dog named after a cat, a grandpa, and a rhythm and blues star. I wish I could be first dog...but, you know, I did have a cookie named after me."

"What are you talking about?" asked Scholar. Giggling, Scout replied, "Girl Scout cookie...you get it?"

Scholar paused then said, "So, do you want to know more about Bo?"

"Yes, I sure do," answered Scout.

Scholar continued with his story, "Bo was born on October 9, 2008, his favorite food is tomatoes, and even though he's a water dog, he doesn't know how to swim yet."

Snubby jumped up shouting, "Swim! I told you never to mention that word again," and he stormed out of the den.

Scholar, with a puzzled and hurt expression, tilted his head to the side and looked at Scout.

Scout knew that this was the time to tell Scholar why he and Snubby ran away from the circus, so in a low voice he begun, "It has to do with the circus. We had been with the circus for about two years. Everything was going fine; my job was to ride a horse, leading Elsa the elephant around the ring. The audience loved it! And Snubby wore a cute little hat and he would pedal around the ring on a little tricycle with the clowns chasing him. One day, the manager had the bright idea that in addition to the human cannon ball act, they would add a canine cannon ball act.

The clowns knew Snubby was a good swimmer because every evening after the circus performance was over, he would show off his swimming abilities in the elephant's water trough. Snubby would dive into the water and retrieve treats that the clowns would throw to him. So they decided to make him the star in the new canine cannon ball act. They would load him into the cannon, shoot him out, and he would land into a large tub of water then swim to the top. He looked like a large sausage flying through the air. Unfortunately, one day when he was shot out of the cannon, he landed in the water and his eye goggles slipped down over his front legs and he couldn't swim, so Elsa came to the rescue, putting her long trunk into the tub and scooping Snubby out.

The audience thought it was part of the act and started clapping. Snubby was so frightened that when the ring master was taking his final bows, Snubby relieved himself right on the ring master's leg. After that, Snubby was put on full-time tiger duty."

Scholar asked, "Tiger duty? What's tiger duty? Did he have to watch the Golf Channel?"

FIRST DOG

Scout giggled and said, "No, no, no, not Tiger the golfer. He had to guard the tigers' cages twenty-four hours a day. You don't know anything about the circus, do you, Scholar?"

Scholar thought, *We have been together for six years, and this is the first time I ever heard anything about those two being with the circus. When we first met, they told me they hitched a ride on a train and just happened to end up in Washington, DC.*

After a brief pause, Scholar asked, "Well, what about you? Why did you leave the circus?"

Scout suddenly realized that he had just slipped up by telling Scholar about their past life with the circus, so he yawned and said, "It's getting late and I think you're tired. We'll talk about it some other time." Scout walked away, shaking his head, as he murmured to himself, "Did he have to watch the Golf Channel?"

The next morning, the day arrived bright and sunny; the light snow that had fallen the day before had been melted by the sun's warmth. Scholar sat proudly waiting for the gang to join him for breakfast. He could hardly wait to show them the pictures he had of the White House Christmas decorations.

When Scout and Snubby entered the den and sat down, Scholar enthusiastically greeted them, "Good morning. Look what I have here. This is an article from the *Washington Post*. The headline reads, 'Bo Is Christmas Star in White House Décor!' The overall holiday theme was 'Shine, Give, Share.' Look at the pictures of the beautiful first lady; she is honoring military families with two large Christmas trees, one decorated with gold stars, for the families of those who have lost loved ones, and the other with blue stars, for families with loved ones that are still serving to protect us. But look at the pictures at the bottom of the page; they put a replica of Bo in almost every room."

6

"Wow! Look at this," Snubby said as he licked his lips and drooled at the picture of a four-hundred-pound ginger-bread White House with Bo sitting on the porch.

In a puzzled voice, Scout said, "Talk about being con-fused. Can you imagine what Bo must have thought, walking around the house and seeing himself everywhere he went?"

Snubby spouted out, "I could deal with that kind of con-fusion if I were first dog."

Scout sighed and said, "They really must love him."

Scholar replied, "'Love' isn't the word for it. The presi-dent thinks Bo is a star and that he is perfect."

"Really?" Scout exclaimed. "It's something extra super-duper special when the president of the United States thinks you're perfect."

Scholar pointed at the newspaper as he said, "And look here…Michelle said she thinks he is the best puppy in the whole wide world."

Snubby huffed, saying, "No wonder she thinks that. The little brown-noser pretends that tomatoes are his favorite food. I bet you he eats those things because of Mommy's healthy eating and her Let's Move campaign."

Scholar replied, "If that's what it takes, it proves a good point; you have to be pretty smart to be the first dog."

Scout piped in, "I'm pretty smart and I have great in-stinct. I knew when it was time to get out of the circus, when they tried to sandwich me between a donkey and a…" As quickly as Scout had piped up, he stopped talking.

Snubby spoke up, finishing his sentence, "A donkey and an elephant. Yeah! I heard you spilling your guts last night, telling Scholar about the tragic mishap with my circus routine. But you never finished the story about what happened to you. Scholar, do you remember last night when Scout told you about how he rode a horse, leading an elephant around the ring?"

"Yes, I do."

Snubby raised his eyebrows. "Well, he didn't tell you the rest of the story. When the circus arrived in Washington, DC, management was changing his act. Instead of him riding around the ring on a horse, they were going to have him ride around the ring on a donkey leading an elephant. When Scout got wind of this, he came whining to me, saying that he wasn't going to be squished between an elephant and a donkey in front of hundreds of people. He screamed, 'Everybody knows that donkeys and elephants do not get along,' he totally freaked out."

Scout interrupted. "Okay! Okay!" he said with a look of embarrassment on his face and then he continued with the story. "So I told Snubby that I'm out of there and that he should go with me, unless he wanted to watch the tigers for the rest of his life. Snubby said he was in, so I told him my plans for our big escape. The circus train was going to pull into Washington, DC's Union Station at eleven in the morning on Monday. What was going to happen was, once the elephants were unloaded from the train, they would be guided on a leisurely stroll to the MCI Center, where the circus was being held. The walk was scheduled to begin at one-thirty.

We already knew that management was going to let the dogs, with some of the clowns and trainers, walk along with the elephants. I told Snubby that earlier I overheard the ring master talking about the exact route we would be taking. With that, it was decided that when we reached Constitution Avenue on the Senate side of the US Capitol, and while the huge crowds were watching the elephants parade down the street, that was where we would make our escape; we would run for our lives.

We caused quite a stir that day, especially when Elsa was trying to follow me, but we made it. You should have seen Snubby that day; his little legs were going as fast as they could. Hey! Snubby, during your little jog that day, I bet you wished that tomatoes had been your favorite food." Snubby stuck his tongue out at Scout and at the same time turned his back to him.

Scholar asked, "How long were you guys on the run before you met me?"

"About three days," said Snubby. "We came across these nice people who worked at the Maine Avenue Fish Market and they gave us food. But one day I heard a customer say that they were going to call the animal shelter; that's when we got scared and decided to move on. Right after that we ran into you behind the Library of Congress."

Puzzled and disappointed, Scholar asked, "Why didn't you ever tell me before about working for the circus? What you told me was that you hitched a ride on a train and you ended up in Washington, DC."

Snubby tucked his head down and said, "We were too embarrassed to tell you that we worked for the circus—you being so smart, knowing all about current events and everything. We couldn't even read very well back then."

Scout looked up at Scholar and said, "That's why we needed your brains to help us find the Fort Totten dump; I kind of remembered what it looked like and the name of it from the year before when the circus was in town. The circus janitor let me ride along with him when he dumped off some garbage. And you are so smart, Scholar; you knew just what to look up so we could find our way there. Yep! Our new address would be forty-nine hundred Bates Road, NE."

At that, the three little pals looked at each other, rubbed their noses together, and reminisced about that day when they all trotted down the street together in search of their new home, singing, "To-the-dump, to-the-dump, to-the-dump-dump-dump!"

Later that evening, Scholar called, "Hey, you guys, come over here for a minute; there is something important I want to talk to you about." When they sat down next to him, he continued, "Ever since we started reading about the first dog, all three of us have been daydreaming about what it would be like to be in that position. And I was thinking that this year, in November, we will have a presidential election, so there is a possibility that we might get a new first family."

Snubby said, "So what are you saying: if there is ever a chance for one of us to be the first dog, this is our best shot at it?"

"That's right, Snubby, but we need more information. We need to know which presidents have had dogs, what kind of dogs they had and what made those dogs so special."

Scout jumped up on top of a crate and proclaimed, "Knowledge is power" then he jumped back down.

With a troubled look on his face, Scholar said, "We need access to a computer."

"A computer!" Snubby shouted. "We don't even have electricity. Did you get a hold of some catnip out there in the dump?"

Scout jumped back up on top of the crate, this time holding his right paw high in the air, and repeated, "Knowledge is power. Anything is possible if you have knowledge."

In a very soft voice, Scholar said, "Mike, the Fort Totten dump manager, has a computer in his office."

"A lot of good that is going to do us," Snubby huffed. "He locks his office when he goes home at night and leaves that yappy little toy poodle in there. She's not fit to be a real watch dog, but that yapping, yapping, yapping, yapping, yapping sound she makes is enough to give any burglar such a bad headache, they wouldn't dare break in; they will run just to get away from that terrible sound."

Scout jumped down from the crate and spoke up. "Pixie doesn't bark when I walk by."

Snubby's head popped up and he said sarcastically, "Pixie! Walk by! Do you mean to say you have been going over to see that yappy little creature, even knowing her name?"

"I only went by a few times," Scout replied.

Puzzled, cocking his head from side to side, Scholar asked, "And she doesn't bark at you?"

Scout sat up proudly with his chest puffed out and said, "Nope! I think she likes me."

"Why do you say that?" Scholar asked in a very inquisitive voice, adding, "I'm thinking that it sounds like someone may have a touch of puppy love."

With a foolish expression, Scout went on to explain, "Well, three times she ran to the door and wagged her tail at me and another time she put her cute little nose against the glass in the window."

With disgust, Snubby said, "Her cute little nose. You have been holding out on us. How long has this been going on, lover boy?"

With a burst of emotion, Scout said, "I feel sorry for her; he leaves her alone night after night and day after day. During the week he's only there from one in the afternoon until five and on Saturdays he comes in early at eight and leaves at three. Who knows what Pixie does on Sundays because the dump is closed? And Mike doesn't even come in to check on her. I don't think he has ever taken her home with him."

In a very secretive manner, Snubby leaned over close to Scout and whispered in his ear, "Well, how does she go to the bathroom?"

"I don't know," Scout replied with disgust. "She's a lady. I am not about to ask her that."

All of a sudden, Scholar had an expression on his face like a light bulb just turned on and he said, "That's it, I got it! Now I know why we call you Scout—you are always paving the way for us, you make sure we get the freshest food from the garbage, and now you're going to get us the computer that we need to do our research."

Scout stuttered, "But, but...how can we do that?"

Snubby quickly said, "What do you mean 'we,' lover boy? It's all up to you and your French connection."

Scout took a deep breath. "I'll try, but I have to make sure that Pixie will trust us." Looking at Snubby, he continued, "If this is going to work, we need to pretend that you can't talk because I need to make sure that no rude comments come out of your mouth."

"Hey! I'll be happy not to talk, lover boy, but am I allowed to grin?"

Scout ignored Snubby's comment and turned to Scholar. "And you need to prove to Pixie how smart you are. By the way, do you know any French?" "Oui, oui, monsieur," he said with a very confident French accent.

CHAPTER 2

The next day, Scout, Snubby, and Scholar went to the shanty where Pixie lived and hid in some bushes that grew nearby. The plan was to patiently wait for a car to drive up. They knew that Mike would have to go outside to talk to the visitors, and that is when Scout could sneak in and talk to Pixie.

Finally a car arrived; as expected, Mike walked out to find out how he could help the passengers. Scout carefully watched and listened to what they were talking about and said, "Perfecto! They have boxes of documents to be shredded; this will give me the time I need to talk to Pixie." As he approached the door, he thought to himself, *I'm in luck; the door is a crack opened.* Using his nose, he nudged the door open and as he entered, he saw Pixie staring at him with a totally shocked look on her face. Quickly, Scout said, "Don't be scared; it's only me" as he dropped the Bo ornament from his mouth.

Pixie batted her eyelashes as she looked into Scout's eyes and asked, "Is that for me?" He nodded yes. She walked over to have a closer look and asked, "What is it?"

Scout was so worried that Mike would return that he nervously blurted out, "It's a Bo ornament but I want you to use it as a door stop and wedge it in the back part of the door, so when Mike leaves today the door will not lock and I can get back in to talk to you."

Confused, Pixie cocked her head from side to side and said, "A Bo ornament…wedge it in the door. What are you talking about?"

Scout looked out the door. "We don't have much time. I think he's coming back. Trust me, Pixie; I'll explain everything to you tonight. Just remember, when Mike leaves tonight, place this in the door jamb; that way, the door will not lock."

Pixie asked, "Are you sure I won't break it?"

As Scout ran out the door, he looked back over his shoulder at her. "Don't worry, that thing is as hard as a rock." She carefully picked up the Bo ornament and pranced away to find a safe hiding place for it.

Scout ran back to where he had left Snubby and Scholar; finding them still in the bushes, he gave them a high-five and said, "Mission accomplished" then they scampered back to camp.

During lunch, Scout told Snubby and Scholar all the details about his brief visit with Pixie. "Look, guys, I think everything will work out fine. I just really hope she is able to wedge that thing in the door without Mike seeing it."

"You'll soon find out," said Scholar, "when you go back at five today."

Five o'clock arrived with Scout hiding outside the manager's office, waiting for him to leave for the day. Sure enough, he heard the door creak as it opened and thought to himself, *Yep, there he goes, right on schedule.* Scout watched as Mike drove down the dusty driveway, got out of his car, and locked the gate. He continued to watch Mike's every move and not until he drove away and was out of sight did Scout make a move.

He was anxious and had a lump in his throat, trying to think of what he would say to Pixie. Scout then trotted over to the front door, saying to himself, *Please open; please open*, as he pushed the door with his nose. Scout was so nervous that he thought he might try to come up with something clever to say when he opened the door, like, "Honey, I'm home," but in a very tentative voice he said, "Hello, Pixie, it's me."

She came around the corner smiling and wagging her tail. "Well, how did I do?"

Scout smiled and said, "You were perfect, Pixie." Looking very proud, Pixie said, "Thanks. Jump up here and have a seat."

The two of them leaped up on the sofa and Scout began to explain what he wanted to talk with her about. He started out by telling her how he chomped down into the Bo ornament and how his friend Scholar knows all about Bo and his life in the White House. Talking a mile a minute, Scout continued to tell Pixie about how he and his buddies wanted a shot at being first dog and because of the presidential election in November; this is now the perfect time.

He went on about how they needed to do research on all the past presidents' dogs and gather information that would help them determine what qualities were needed to be first dog. Scout took a deep breath and continued, "So in other words, to do our research and gather all of this information, we need to use Mike's computer."

Pixie looked at him with her big brown eyes and said, "No promises Scout, I will need to meet with your friends first. We can meet tomorrow after Mike leaves. But, I'm confused; do you think that Bo is just waiting to be kicked out of his home?"

"No, no, no, Pixie, we love Bo. He's the best first dog ever. But this is an election year and you never know what can happen during an election year."

Sternly, Pixie explained, "You know, Scout, you don't have to live in the White House to be a first dog. There are a lot of people out there, who have dogs, and those people think their dogs are first dogs and they treat them that way; they love them just as they are. And another thing, when you research the presidential dogs, I think you should do research about other dogs, too. Did you know that dogs took over the box office at the movie theaters this year? Just to name a couple, Uggie, the Jack Russell in *The Artist*, and a fox terrier named Snowy in *The Adventures of Tintin* were stars. In my eyes, these dogs are also top dogs, first dogs, or whatever you want to call them."

Scout squirmed. "I agree...those are some very good points."

Pixie said, "I have a question: in order to get yourself adopted, how do you plan on meeting the potential presidents?"

Scout looked down at the floor and in a mild manner said, "We haven't figured that part out yet," but then he raised his voice to a very confident level and said, "Knowledge is power, and speaking of knowledge, how did you know about those dogs that were in the movies this year? I know Mike doesn't get the newspaper."

With sad eyes, Pixie looked up and said, "I saw it on some web page. It gets very lonely being shut up in here, so I bring the world in to me."

Scout felt really sad about Pixie being lonely, but on the other hand, he was jumping for joy inside. And couldn't wait to tell his buddies the news, that she knows how to use the computer. Scout snuggled close to Pixie and said, "I promise you won't ever have to worry about being lonely again." After saying that, he wondered if that was a promise he could keep, but deep down he knew he would figure out a way — just like he would figure out how he would be the first dog.

CHAPTER 3

The following day, just like clockwork, at 5:00 PM sharp, Mike headed out the door to go home. Scout was there, too, waiting, and when the coast was clear, only then did he lead his buddies to the door. But before he pushed open the door, there were some last-minute instructions for Snubby: "No burping, don't pass gas, smile, and remember you can't talk."

Snubby grunted, "I am smiling...I'm smiling on the inside. My face always looks like this. You expect too much from an English bull dog."

Scout was smiling as he turned and nudged the door open. Entering, he called out, "Pixie, it's us."

Pixie was sitting on the sofa when they walked in, but quickly jumped down and approached Scout.

"Pixie, this is Snubby, and um...um...um, he doesn't know how to talk."

With a very sympathetic expression, Pixie walked over and stood very close to Snubby, then as loud as she could, she shouted in his ear, "Nice to meet you, Tubby."

Snubby cringed and dropped back on his hind legs, his behind hitting the floor with a thump.

Quickly, Scout said, "No! No! Pixie, his name is Snubby and he's not deaf; he just can't talk."

Pixie hung her head and said in a meek little voice, "Sorry, Snubby." *Gosh, I feel so stupid*, she thought. *I need to make a comeback so they will know how smart I really am.*

Scout then turned to Scholar. "Pixie, I would like to introduce you to Scholar."

At that, and with a thick French accent, Scholar bowed and said, "Salute, mademoiselle."

Pixie raised her head high and in a sober tone replied, "And hello to you. However, I am not French. I am German. Most people believe the poodle originated in France, but in reality the word 'poodle' is a derivative of the German word 'pudel,' which is the short form of the word 'pudelhund,' meaning 'water dog.' "

Scholar was totally shocked by Pixie's correction. He thought to himself for a second, then in a wonderful German dialect uttered, "Guten tag, fraulein."

Pixie was not the least bit impressed and replied, "English, please. English is my first language."

Scout was very anxious; the introductions did not go as expected. Pausing for a moment, he then said, "It looks as though we are going to have a pretty good team here."

With that, Pixie gestured in a hospitable manner for everyone to please have a seat. Everyone found a comfortable spot. Scout began recapping the purpose of the meeting—the information collection—and how important the computer would be to their success.

Pixie spoke up, "I have a lot to lose if Mike finds out about us doing this. We must be very structured; that is the only way I will agree to this."

"Structured? What exactly do you mean?" Scholar asked.

"I mean we need a plan to clearly define our roles, and since we only have one computer, we will have to schedule the time each of us will work."

Scholar was very pleased with her and the way she was thinking. "Wow! Pixie, you're right. What great ideas you have; you can be the secretary."

"The secretary!" she howled, furious. She was sure that her snowy white coat must have turned a bright shade of pink. Scout wanted to calm Pixie down, but before he could say anything, she wailed, "I will be the supervisor, assigning your work hours and tasks. I will be the trainer, instructing you on how to efficiently surf the Internet and telling you which web sites will be the most helpful. And last but not least, I will be the computer technician, fixing all computer-related problems and fixing your mistakes."

Meanwhile, Snubby was so keyed up and nervous, with not being able to say anything that he let out a loud burp but with the heat of the discussion going on, and to his relief, no one seemed to notice.

The conversation ended with Scout and Scholar looking at one another at exactly the same time, saying, "We agree with you, Pixie."

This brought Snubby to his feet; he could not believe his ears. He glared at Scholar and Scout and started scratching his ears, first with one paw then the other; he didn't know what else to do because he wasn't allowed to talk and this was his form of sign language to try to let them know that he couldn't believe his ears.

In a soft, kind voice, Pixie said, "Thanks for understanding; I promise I'll keep everything organized, so you can get the information you need as soon as possible." She then turned and looked at Snubby, who was still scratching non-stop, harder and harder. Pixie just had to ask, "Does he have fleas?"

Scholar gave Snubby the 'knock-it-off' look and replied, "No, no, no, he has a touch of dry skin due to the winter climate." Pixie nodded her head in agreement and quickly said, "Just one last question: are you all house-broken?"

At that, Snubby abruptly stopped scratching and stared at Scholar.

Scout spoke up and said, "Yes."

She turned to Scholar and said, "You are the data analyst" and then directed her attention to Scout and Snubby: "You two will be the data and information collectors. Since there is only one computer, Scout and Snubby will work on shifts. Snubby, your hours are from midnight until seven in the morning. Scout, you will work from five in the evening until midnight."

Snubby was so furious he could hardly contain himself; he kept biting his upper lip with his little jagged teeth, thinking to himself, *Okay, Scout, my little buddy, your day is coming.* Pixie continued, "Scholar and I will work the five-until-midnight shift along with Scout, and of course I will be available if Snubby needs help during his shift."

Scout and Scholar started a side conversation, but Pixie interrupted: "I'm not quite finished yet. Tomorrow, which is Saturday, we will all meet at four for training. Mike leaves at three, so everything should work out just fine."

"Training? What kind of training?" asked Scout.

Quickly, Pixie responded, "How to use the computer and do data collection. My friends, data collection and its integrity can be very tricky. For example, Scholar read in the *Washington Post* that the first family left town to spend the remainder of the holidays in Hawaii, Bo and the president were not with them. What really happened was, the president stayed home and left a few days later; this was after he took Bo to Pet Smart to do some Christmas shopping. The newspapers had to correct the story."

Scholar looked at Pixie with admiration and said, "I could sure use some training." Everyone was happy with the plan of action except for Snubby.

Pixie walked them to the door and said, "Goodnight. See you tomorrow at four sharp."

As soon as they walked outside, Snubby growled, "I can't believe the mess you got me into! I felt like I was in an Army boot camp with a little French-German Sergeant barking orders at me left and right."

Scholar said, "Calm down. Pixie is very organized and I believe she is trying her best to help us make the very best use of our time."

Scout chimed in, "Remember there is only one computer, and if anyone needs to be organized, it's the three of us."

CHAPTER 4

The next day at 4:00 PM on the dot, they arrived at Pixie's. She greeted them at the door. "Hi, I'm so excited. Look over here at how I have everything organized."

Snubby was standing behind her, moving his mouth, mimicking her every word.

Scholar gave Snubby the evil eye as he said, "You must have been up all night preparing for our lesson. We really appreciate it."

First, she showed them how to log on to the computer and how to set up files. They were so excited; this was the first time they had ever used a computer. She then explained her plan for the first phase of the data research.

"We have had forty-four presidents from the year 1789 to the present. Snubby, you will research all of the presidents for first dogs, taking the first through the twenty-second. And Scout will take the twenty-third through the forty-forth. Here is a copy of the list for each of you. Now don't get confused when you see Grover Cleveland's name; he is on both lists. He was the twenty-second president from 1885 through 1889 as a Republican and the twenty-fourth when he returned to office in 1893 as a Democrat, serving until 1897."

Puzzled, Scout said, "I never heard of such a thing. I always thought you were either an elephant or a donkey. How could he be both?"

Pixie laughed. "Scout, you may find the answer to your question during your research. When you do, let us know."

Scholar was sitting on the edge of his seat, waiting to hear how his data analysis function would fit into the plan "Um, pardon me, Pixie, but how do I fit in?"

"I saved the best part for last. You will go into the information files created by Snubby and Scout and analyze the data, looking for common threads among all of the first dogs."

Scholar smiled. "That will help us understand what it takes to be first dog. Perfecto!"

Pixie went on showing Scout and Snubby how they would gather their information. She logged on to Google and typed in "winner of Westminster Dog Show 2012" then hit enter. Very proudly, she said, "Look here, there are many data results, but I'm going to select this one."

"Why select that one?" Scout asked.

"That's a good question. This one is from a national newspaper and, many times, their information is much more reliable." She hit enter and up popped a picture of Malachi, a beautiful Pekingese who took best in show.

Wide-eyed, Scout exclaimed, "How beautiful."

Pixie quickly informed Scout, "A poodle won best in show in 1991 and 2002."

Snubby just laughed to himself, thinking, *In addition to all of her other wonderful qualities, she also has a jealous streak.*

Pixie cautioned, "There is one last thing: I want you to keep an open mind when doing your research. You will soon discover that there are other dogs that have made a great contribution to the canine race. When you come across them, look at what made them special."

Snubby was tapping his foot, thinking to himself, *By the time she finishes with me, I'm not even going to have a mind.*

They worked diligently through the month of January. Other than a few temper tantrums from Snubby, everything was going smoothly. Pixie scheduled a check point meeting for the first Sunday in February at 9:00 AM to discuss what information had been collected and analyzed to date.

The morning of the meeting, Scholar called Snubby, telling him it was time to get up or he would be late. Snubby looked up with his eyes half open and moaned, "I'm sick. I can't go."

"Yes, you can go. You're not sick." Snubby cried, "I can't...she's driving me crazy."

"So what did Pixie do to you now?"

Impersonating Pixie, Snubby said, "'Do this, Snubby, do that, Snubby. What are you doing out there, Snubby? I can't hear that click, click, clicking on the keyboard.' Last night I even had a nightmare about her; she wanted me to give her a pedicure. Yeah, I'll give her a pedicure alright. I'll gnaw her little pom-poms right off."

"How can you say such a terrible thing?" Scholar frowned. "This is a very important day and, for your information, Pixie told me that you are doing an excellent job."

Surprised, Snubby lifted his head. "Really?"

"Yes, she worries about you because you are up all night working by yourself." Snubby yawned, leisurely stretched, and proceeded to get ready for the meeting.

All the way there, Snubby kept belting out a strange sound. Scholar thought, *Maybe he really is sick*, so he asked, "Snubby, why are you making that terrible sound?"

"Oh! I'm practicing my Barack bark."

"Your Barack bark? What are you talking about? You sound like a cat throwing up a hair ball," exclaimed Scout.

"Listen, it goes like this: Bar-r-r-rack! It just rolls off the tip of my tongue. That's how I'm going to greet the prez when I meet him. I want to be able to address him in a respectable manner." Scholar and Scout could only shake their heads at one another.

Pixie was excited, pacing back and forth at the door, waiting for them.

Outside the door, Snubby whispered to Scout, "How come she never comes out of the house?"

Scout shook his head sadly. "I don't know."

"Hello, everyone, please come in." Scout gave Pixie a little peck on the cheek. Blushing, she said, "This is a big day. Let's see how you did with your data research."

Scholar started out by commending Scout and Snubby on their findings and began his report. "Twenty-five of America's forty-three presidents..." He glanced at Pixie and said, "I'm not counting Grover Cleveland twice...have had dogs while they were in office. Some of them have had many dogs, for example, George Washington had thirty-six foxhounds, according to Snubby's data."

Scout chimed in, "Not only was he the father of our nation, he's also the father of the American foxhounds."

Scholar continued, "Some other presidents have had as many as seven to twelve dogs, but the majority had six dogs or less."

Pixie asked Scholar, "What type of dogs did the presidents have?"

"Well, according to the research, all different breeds. However, for today's meeting, I compiled a list of the presidents that had bull dogs, Springer spaniels, and, last but not least, mutts."

"What about poodles?"

"Pixie, I even sorted that information out just for you. Grover Cleveland was said to have had a poodle, but the data I read didn't have its name."

Scout smiled and winked at Pixie. "I bet the name was Pixie."

"Teddy Roosevelt had a mutt named Skip."

Scout chimed in with laughter, "He's the president who also had another dog, a bull terrier, who almost caused an international scandal when he ripped off the French ambassador's pants during a White House function." Everybody broke out into laughter, except for Snubby, who thought, *All I can do is sit here looking stupid because I have to pretend I can't talk.*

Scholar went on, "Warren Harding had a bull dog named Oh Boy; he also had an Airedale named Laddie Boy, who had his own chair to sit in during cabinet meetings." Snubby huffed, saying to himself, *That figures, the bull dog has to lie on the floor.*

"And look, Snubby, we have another bull dog. He belonged to Calvin Coolidge and his name was Boston Beans." Everyone looked at Snubby and giggled. "Next we have a mutt named Feller, belonging to Harry Truman."

Pixie interjected, "Wasn't he the president that said, 'If you want a friend in Washington, get a dog?' "

"That's exactly right," said Scholar before continuing. "Sorry, you guys, but we have another mutt here; it looks like the mutts are outnumbering you. Yuki was a mixed-breed dog found by Lyndon Johnson's daughter at a gas station in Texas and was famous for disgracing... Let's move on to the next one."

"No, finish," Pixie insisted.

"Okay...disgracing everyone that was present in the Oval Office when he took a leak in front of the shah of Iran. And later he bit a White House police officer in the groin."

Scout crinkled up his nose. "Ouch! I wonder what the police officer ever did to him."

Looking at Pixie, Scholar said, "This is the last poodle on my list; her name was Vicky, and she belonged to Richard Nixon."

Scout then voiced, "He's the president that also had a dog named Checkers. I'm currently doing research on Checkers. I'll have some great information about him at our next meeting."

"And for our final mutt of the day, we have Gritts, who was a gift from Jimmy Carter to his daughter, Amy."

Scout was sitting with a sad look on his face; there had been no mention of any presidents having had a Springer spaniel.

Then Scholar spoke up, "Saving the best for last, but not least, it looks like we have a couple of celebrity Springer spaniels; they belonged to the Bushes. Millie, who belonged to George H., was the author of a book that sold more copies than the autobiography of the president himself. And his son George W. also had a Springer spaniel named Spot; he was named after Scott Fletcher, a former Texas Ranger baseball player."

Now Scout was smiling from ear to ear. "I have a question: how do you get 'Spot' out of 'Scott Fletcher'? Is this bad data collected, or is it another one of those Bo Diddley things?"

"No, no, no, silly," said Pixie. "When they got Spot as a puppy, Bush owned the Texas Rangers, so he named his dog Spot Fletcher Bush."

All of a sudden headlights from a car were shining through the window; panicked, thinking it might be Mike, Pixie screamed, "Hide!" *Hide?* They thought. *Hide where?* Scholar ran behind the sofa; Snubby and Scout saw what appeared to be an open pantry door and ran in. Once inside, they spotted a cat's litter box.

Snubby anxiously looked around the room. "Let the games begin! A cat must live here."

Scout went, "Shhhh" as he walked over to examine the paw print in the litter box. "That's Pixie's paw print."

In a not so quiet voice, Snubby blurted out, "I always wondered where she did her business."

Just as he said that, Pixie raced around the corner. "What are you two doing in here?"

Scout shrugged his shoulders. "You told us to hide."

She was so embarrassed she couldn't look either one of them in the eye. "Well, sorry, it was a false alarm" and she trotted away, thinking to herself, *I can't believe they saw that litter box. How embarrassing. And Snubby can talk! I'm going to get to the bottom of this. Poor Snubby, all these nights he sat in silence.*

When the meeting reconvened, they discussed what they would do if a car drove up unexpectedly again; they didn't want to panic next time. Pixie showed them the one-way (out) doggie door at the back of the house. She told them that Mike had installed it so she could escape if there was ever a fire.

Pixie wrapped up the meeting, telling them what a great job they did over the past month and how proud she was of them. She went on to explain, "The next part of data collection will be very time-consuming as you gather specific traits and other interesting facts about the first dogs."

Scout spoke up, saying, "Snubby is already practicing his interesting trait. Snubby, let her hear your Barack greeting."

He held his head up high and barked, "Bar-r-r-rack." Pixie, smiled, thinking, *You do that quite well for someone that can't talk*, and then she leaned over and gave him a nudge of encouragement. "That was great; it almost sounds just like his name."

She then continued with the work plan. "So today is February fifth." Reaching down and showing Snubby the calendar, she asked, "When do you think we should meet?"

He looked up at her, wagging his tail, and pointed to Sunday, February 19. Pixie felt bad for Snubby; he had worked so hard and was barely included in today's meeting because supposedly he couldn't talk. This was the first time she had ever seen Snubby so happy. "That date is a good choice. Instead of waiting for a whole month, we can meet in two weeks. Then we'll see what facts we have and determine what else is needed. Do you all think the same time is good?" Everyone nodded in agreement and said their goodnights.

As they walked home that evening, they were so excited, talking about how well the meeting had gone. Snubby couldn't get over how Pixie let him pick the next meeting date. "She probably did that to get on my good side because I saw that pitiful litter box she uses."

Scholar questioned, "What litter box?"

They told him the whole story: how they went to find a hiding place when the car drove up and discovered the litter box, then Pixie walked in and wanted to know what they were doing back there. "And to top it off, old big mouth over there," Scout said, gesturing to Snubby, "pops out with, 'I always wondered where she did her business.' "

In his own defense, Snubby said, "I was shocked. I have never heard of such a thing as a dog using a kitty litter box."

CHAPTER 5

For the next two weeks, they searched for specific traits, personalities, and interesting stories about the remaining first dogs. Because Snubby wouldn't talk, Pixie decided to give him some help; she would work with him every night during his shift, even volunteering to give the oral presentation of his findings at the upcoming meeting. *For sure*, she thought, *he has to tell me the truth about being able to talk.* But, no, not a word came out of Snubby; he just grinned and bared it.

Back at the den, Scout and Scholar were discussing Snubby, about how surprised they were that he had not had anything bad to say about Pixie in the past two weeks.

On Sunday, and right on schedule, the gang showed up for the meeting at Pixie's. When everyone was inside and settled, Pixie started. "Okay! What we'll do is go around the room, each of us telling what they found about their first dogs—something notable, something that stood out. As we do this, make a mental note of the unique traits that you think these first dogs had, and then we will discuss them later."

Scholar nodded in agreement, and then asked, "What about Snubby and his stories?"

Pixie stared at Snubby. "I will help him with that."

Scout, smiling at Pixie, said, "Let's go in the order of the presidents, that means you're first."

Pixie again stared at Snubby, and then walked up to him and said so everyone could hear, "The charade is over. I know you can talk. I overheard you. Now why in the world would you do something so dumb?"

Scout spoke up, "It's all my fault. I talked Snubby into not talking. Not knowing you, but knowing Snubby, who can at times be grumpy and crude in his ways, I thought it best that he say nothing so we could gain your confidence."

Snubby spoke up, "Well, for one thing, I am glad you finally know. I thought I was going to lose my mind, and you're too nice to keep fooling."

They all thought that Pixie was owed an apology and, looking at each other, said in unison, "We are sorry, Pixie. Will you forgive us?"

Pixie was thinking that these three should take their show on the road, which brought a smile to her face. "I will give you guys one more chance. Now, Snubby, get up there and give your report."

Snubby was in shock but began, "Thomas Jefferson had working sheepdogs and they watched over his flock of sheep. He was so serious about keeping them safe that he once hanged a dog for attacking one of his sheep."

At that, Scout cringed. "I sure hope that dog wasn't a sheepdog."

Snubby only shrugged his shoulders and continued. "Next, James Buchanan had Lara, a Newfoundland; she would lay motionless for hours, with one eye open and the other closed, always keeping that open eye on the president. Then we have Ulysses Grant; his son's dog was also a Newfoundland named Faithful. In the past, his son had other dogs, but for some weird reason they kept dying, so with this dog, the president told every White House employee, 'If this dog dies, every one of you will be fired.' "

Snubby paused and Scholar spoke up, "Continue on. What else do you have?"

"Continue? That's it! President's number one through twenty-two did not have first dogs with a lot of interesting information. However, if you want to know about the alligator John Quincy Adams kept in the White House bathroom or the pet elephant that James Buchanan had, you're in luck."

Scout yelled, "What do you mean he had an elephant? He was a Democrat. No wonder poor little Lara would lie there with one eye open; she was afraid that elephant would squish the president."

Laughing, Snubby went on. "I don't know why he had an elephant, or why Calvin Coolidge, who was a Republican, had a donkey named Ebenezer."

Scout could only shake his head in disbelief. *Don't go there*, Snubby was thinking. *Your girlfriend is going to find out what a sissy you are when it comes to donkeys and elephants.*

"It's your turn, Scout," Scholar said. "What have you found?"

Scout was still out of sorts because of what happened earlier in the meeting and was worried that Pixie would be mad at him. He took a minute to gather his thoughts. "At the last meeting, we already touched on some of the facts about the first dogs I have been researching. So today I will report the new information I have found." His voice was cracking as he continued, "Laddie Boy, an Airedale that belonged to Warren Harding, would invite all the neighborhood dogs to the White House for his birthday parties, where they dined on dog biscuit birthday cake. They even have a statue of him at the Smithsonian."

Snubby licked his lips, thinking, *I can't wait to be first dog.*

"Next we have Fala, a Scottish terrier who belonged to Franklin D. Roosevelt. The president had a bunch of other dogs, but Fala was the love of his life. This first dog was the star of an MGM Hollywood movie about the typical day of a dog in the White House. Fala also became an honorary army private, and received the honor by contributing one dollar to the war effort. A sculpture of Fala is also in the Roosevelt Memorial."

Pixie could see that Scout was distracted; he was skipping over facts and acting like he could not wait to be finished with his report. She piped in, "So far I think Fala is my role model."

Scout said, "Then next…" as he pawed through his paperwork, dropping half of it on the floor, "John Kennedy was the first president to request that his dogs meet him at the presidential helicopter when he arrived at the White House."

Scout was talking faster and faster, not giving anyone a chance to comment on his stories. "One of his dogs was a mutt named Pushinka, a gift from Soviet Premier Khrushchev. She was the daughter of the Russian space dog Strelka. Pushinka liked to climb up a ladder to a tree house that belonged to the president's daughter, Caroline. Lyndon Johnson loved his beagles, named Him and Her. However, the president got in trouble with the media when he once picked Him up by his ears; that picture was in every newspaper in the country. The two beagles even appeared on the cover of *Life* magazine."

Snubby was squirming, raising his front leg. Scout ignored him; he just wanted to finish and sit down, but Snubby was persistent and so he finally asked, "Do you have a question?"

"Yeah, let's go back to that thing about the ears; don't you think that might have hurt?"

"That's what everyone in America thought but the president said the dog loved it." Scout continued, "Now here is a great trait a first dog should have: Johnson's collie, Blanco, always shook hands with the president whenever he left and returned to the White House. And finally we have Richard Nixon; he had a cocker spaniel named Checkers. This dog even has a special day named after him, 'Checkers Day,' which is also known as 'Dogs in Politics Day.' Nixon was a candidate for vice president, running with Dwight Eisenhower. On September 23, 1952, he gave a speech..."

Scout abruptly stopped and looked at the group. "I don't feel very well. Do you mind if I give you each a copy of the rest of my report and you can read it later?"

Quickly, Pixie said, "No, we don't mind, do we, guys? But don't forget our next group meeting is scheduled for March fourth." Snubby and Scholar both shook their heads in agreement and got up to leave, taking a copy of Scout's report with them.

Before Scout could leave, Pixie grabbed him and pulled him aside. "I would like you to stay." Scout felt so bad that all he could do was hang his head. "Scout, look at me. You're the best friend anyone could ever have and I know you only had my best interest at heart. And I'm in love you."

This got Scout's attention. With his head spinning and heart pounding, he started to say something, but Pixie quickly stopped him. "Let's never talk about this Snubby thing again. Now, go!"

As Scout was leaving, he kissed Pixie goodnight and whispered in her ear, "I love you, too, Pixie."

CHAPTER 6

The next day when Snubby arrived, Pixie told him she was sorry if she embarrassed him yesterday, but just didn't understand why he had been silent for the past six weeks. "I thought perhaps you didn't like me."

Snubby searched for the right words, blurting out, "Well, you are a little bossy, telling everyone what to do all the time, but I do like you."

"I didn't mean to be bossy; I just know from experience that if you don't have a plan, bad things can happen."

Snubby cocked his head to the side, asking, "What kind of bad things?"

Pixie looked up with tears in her eyes. "This may take a while and please don't tell anyone. It happened when my human family moved from Chicago to Washington, DC. We arrived at the airport and I was in a doggie carrier waiting for them to pick me up at the luggage claim area

Normally when we traveled, they came and got me right away. This time there must have been some kind of confusion. I waited and waited and then some guy wearing a hoodie snatched me up and ran out the door. He tried to sell me, but I was crying and shaking so badly that no one wanted me.

After two days, he just dropped me off on a street corner. I had no idea where I was or where to go. That's when I met Mike. I saw him get out of his car to close and lock a gate. I ran over to him whimpering. Mike picked me up in his arms and brought me here to live."

Snubby was shocked by Pixie's story; he sat there with his mouth wide open, finally asking, "And how long ago was that?"

She thought a minute. "It's been about three years now. He means well but doesn't know about the attention a poodle requires. He gives me food, if he's in the mood he talks to me, and you saw that little door he put in so I could get out in case of an emergency."

Snubby, even though uncomfortable, let his curiosity get the best of him, so in a clumsy manner he asked, "But why does he make you use a litter box? The emergency door should allow you to go out when you need to and come back in when you're ready."

Hanging her head in embarrassment, she defended Mike. "It's not his fault. Originally he had the door set up that way. I'm just afraid to go outside. So he got me the litter box to use."

"You mean to say you never go outside! But why?"

Pixie broke down crying. "I'm afraid! I'm…I'm afraid somebody might get me again."

Snubby had no idea how to handle a crying female; he was squirming and trying to think of something he could say that would comfort her. Finally he approached her and said, "Here…put your head on my shoulder."

They sat together like that until she stopped crying. Then in a nostalgic tone, Pixie started telling Snubby about her life before all of this happened. "I miss my family. Mommy was so sweet to me; she used to call me her 'little Lovie.' She never had a cross word to say to anyone, except when Daddy would watch television with me and feed me peanuts, yelling, 'Go, Bears!' I didn't know what he was yelling about; there was just a bunch of grown men on television, running around knocking each other down, and I didn't see a bear in sight."

Snubby smiled, but he was still out of his comfort zone. He could tell Pixie was feeling better so he asked, "Think we should get back to work, my cute little friend?"

Pixie sniffled, managed a little smile, and nodded yes. She pleaded, "Snubby, please don't tell anyone about this yet."

For the next two weeks, the gang continued to do their research about other noteworthy dogs. Snubby never said a word to anyone about Pixie's story.

Today was the day of the big meeting and the day that Pixie had been looking forward to. She always thought that being first dog was important but she wanted her friends to know that other dogs, in their own ways, are just as special.

Scholar began with his report on dogs that served in the military. "Since World War I, dogs have helped soldiers fight for our freedom and have saved many lives. Remember when the Navy Seals stormed Osama bin Laden's hideout in Pakistan? They had with them one four-legged soldier named Cairo."

"Wow! I never knew that," Scout exclaimed, then asked, "How many military dogs does the United States have?"

Scholar looked through his notes. "As of 2010, the army had over twenty-eight hundred dogs; they are even outfitted with their own specialized gear. In World War II, Chips, a German shepherd-collie-husky mix — a mutt, just like me," he chuckled, "broke away from his handler and attacked a gun shelter containing an enemy machine gun crew in Sicily. He seized one man and forced the entire crew to surrender. And then we have USMC Sergeant Stubby, a hero and veteran of World War I."

Snubby sat up proudly. "Did you say Snubby?"

Scholar looked at him, shaking his head no as he proceeded to carefully enunciate, "Stubby was known for his chunky body and..." Everyone had burst into laughter. Scholar said, "Okay, you guys, be quiet. It gets even better...and his ability to alert the soldiers when there were gas attacks; he could smell the gas in time for the soldiers to get their masks on." Over the roars of laughter, he spoke louder, "One time he captured a German spy by the seat of his pants."

Scout was now rolling around on the floor laughing, as he said, "If he was anything like our Snubby, I bet they had plenty of gas drills."

Pixie contained her laughter, saying, "Stop picking on Snubby."

Snubby let the jokes roll right off his back, interjecting, "Oh, yeah! I remember Woodrow Wilson didn't have any dogs when he was president but I read that he shook hands with Stubby after he captured that German spy."

The discussion then lead to other service dogs they had read about, like police dogs who help police officers on duty, accelerant dogs who help firemen determine the source of the fire, agriculture detector dogs who are used for finding illegal plants or other agricultural products, seeing eye dogs for the blind, and therapy dogs who visit people in hospitals and nursing homes. The boys thought to themselves, *Pixie was absolutely right. All of these dogs are awesome!*

"Let's move on to Hollywood," Pixie said with excitement. "These are my two favorite Hollywood top dogs: Rin Tin Tin and Lassie.

Rin Tin Tin appeared in thirty films from 1922 until 1931. He had a diamond-studded collar, his own production unit, limo and driver, and ate steak prepared by his personal chef."

Snubby licked his lips. "I love steak."

Pixie continued, "Hold on to your hats, everyone. Wait until you hear the Hollywood gossip I have about Lassie. Eight generations of Lassies have thrilled families since the 1943 movie *Lassie Come Home*. She was trained and groomed for the silver screen. But Lassie, the world's most famous collie, is also the world's best female impersonator: Lassie was a male, and his real name was Pal. In addition, Pal's descendants who played Lassie were also males."

Snubby was disgusted. Just the thought of this made his stomach churn; he had always had a crush on Lassie. Quickly his thinking went to the big story he wanted to talk about, and while scratching his head, he said, "Oh, yeah! I have a story. There was this cool German shepherd named Highball, the only witness during the Saint Valentine's Day Massacre."

Skeptical, Scout said, "Are you making this up?"

"No," Snubby said as he leaned in closer to the group. "There were these two Chicago gangs, South Side Italians, led by Al Capone, and the North Side Irish, led by Bugs Morgan. On the morning of February fourteenth, 1929, Capone hired some gangsters to pay a little visit to the garage where Morgan and his gang were meeting. The gangsters, dressed as police officers, burst into the garage, the seven people inside were lined up against the wall, and Bang! Bang! Bang! Bang!

While this was going on, poor Highball was in the garage tied to a truck, barking and howling. The people from a boarding house across the street came to see what was upsetting the dog. Did they get an eye full when they opened that garage door! To this day when dogs walk past the area where that wall used to stand, they sometimes, bark, howl, and whine in fear."

Scholar asked, "That was a really interesting story, but what does it have to do with these other talented dogs we have been discussing?"

Shrugging his shoulders, Snubby replied, "I don't know. I just thought it would be a nice, scary story to tell before we walked home in the dark."

CHAPTER 7

Pixie looked at the calendar; *I can't believe how fast the past two and a half months have flown by,* she thought. *This will be our fourth official meeting, March 18* and she marked it on the calendar. *I have been so happy, having my new friends keeping me company. Our crazy work schedules have one of them always coming or going.*

Then her thoughts went to Scout. *He is so sweet, bringing me presents almost daily.* Smiling, she thought, *And that big heart-shaped box of cookies he brought me for Valentine's Day; it was so large he could hardly carry it.* Shaking her head with amazement, she thought how cute he was and that he always found the best things. *Yep! Just like my Bo ornament. We are so lucky that the Bo ornament is still working to keep the door from locking.*

Then her happy thoughts turned into worrisome thoughts. *What would happen if Mike found out? What's going to happen when we are finished collecting all the information? If I don't see them anymore, I will really miss them.* And then she recalled what Scout told her two and a half months ago: "I promise you won't ever have to worry about being lonely again." All of a sudden she heard a familiar sound; it was Snubby practicing his "Barack" greeting.

As he approached the door, Pixie ran to greet him. "What are you doing here this time of day? You were up all night working and you should be home sleeping."

Yawning, Snubby dropped the package he was carrying and replied, "Well, I have some great prime rib I want you to try. I also need to look something up on the Internet before Mike gets here at one."

"Thanks so much, this looks delish! Help yourself to the computer." Pixie sat down and munched on her treat as Snubby tapped away on the keyboard.

"This can't be," he exclaimed.

With her mouth full of food, Pixie mumbled, "What can't be?"

"The cherry blossoms! The flowers will be peaking sooner than I thought. On the first of March, the official forecasters predicted that the blossoms would be at their peak from March twenty-fourth through March thirty-first. And now the final prediction reports the peak for blooming will fall between March twentieth and March twenty-third!"

Pixie stopped eating, trotted over to the computer, jumped up, and sat down next to Snubby. "What's a cherry blossom look like? Let me see." Snubby pulled up a picture of the 2011 cherry blossom trees that ring Washington's tidal basin. Pixie gasped. "Look at all of those beautiful pink and white flowers! What kind of trees did you say they were?"

"They are Japanese Yoshino cherry blossom trees, and this year they will celebrate the hundredth birthday of the cherry blossoms. Tokyo gave us three thousand of these trees as a gift in 1912."

Concerned that Snubby was disappointed, she asked, "Why are you so upset about the date the blossoms will peak?"

Pouting, Snubby said, "Because I go every year to see them. This is my favorite time of the year. Last year they peaked on March twenty-ninth, and the year before it was March thirty-first. And read this; it says this is the earliest time they have peaked in the last seven years."

Trying to console Snubby, Pixie calmly said, "You can still go and see the blossoms. Today is the sixteenth; you have four days."

Snubby looked up at Pixie. "Really? What about all the research we still have to do?"

"The research can wait. We are ahead of schedule, and you deserve a special day off."

Snubby was wagging his tail; he leaned over, kissing Pixie on the cheek, as he jokingly said, "I hope my little buddy Scout didn't see me do that."

Pixie blushed. "Well, it's getting late. Mike should be here soon, and you, Mr. King of the Cherry Blossoms, need to go home and get some sleep."

Snubby was jumping with joy; he couldn't wait to get home and tell Scout and Scholar the good news. As he was walking home, he was thinking about his grumpy personality and emotions. He couldn't understand how he could be so disappointed about the cherry blossoms and then seconds later be so happy. He came to the conclusion that he would have to start seeing his water bowl as half full instead of half empty and try to overcome his grumpy nature. He nodded his head, affirming his decision, and continued walking home.

"I took Pixie her prime rib; she loved it and I found the cherry blossom information on the web."

Scholar looked up and said "That's great. So what day are you going to take your sabbatical to see the blossoms this year?"

Snubby replied, "March twentieth."

Scout's head popped up. "Wow! They sure are early this year."

Scholar pulled out the newspaper. "I read that the warm winter and early fall we had last year would cause many plants and flowers to bloom early. As you know, this whole winter has been unseasonably warm."

"So, guys, what time should we leave that beautiful morning, on the first day of spring?" Snubby inquired.

Scout spoke up, "We can't leave Pixie alone; we're still doing research. That's just two days after our meeting."

Confident in his reply, Snubby said, "Pixie is going with us; she just doesn't know it yet."

Scout stammered, "But…but she won't even go outside of her own door. How are we going to get her to go to the tidal basin?"

"I don't know yet. We have until our meeting on Sunday to figure it out, and we will need to convince her at our meeting," Snubby said, and then he headed to bed.

Over the next two days, they discussed different ideas they each had to persuade Pixie to go outside, and finally came up with a game plan they all agreed on. On Sunday morning they arrived at Pixie's; as usual she was delighted to see them and began reading the agenda.

With a sense of urgency in his voice, Scout interrupted, "Pixie we have another agenda item we would like to discuss today. We care about you very much and are concerned that if there was an emergency, you would be too afraid to go outside through the escape door Mike put in for you."

Pixie was bewildered. "I...I, um, would definitely go outside."

Scout began walking toward the door. "Okay, Pixie, let's have a fire drill and watch you go out."

She froze in her tracks. "I can't. I'm afraid."

Scout asked, "Afraid of what?"

Pixie just stared at the door. Snubby spoke up, "She's afraid of being abducted, and don't ask. Let me handle this." Scout thought, *Abducted? What is he talking about?* But he didn't say a word.

"What I need is for you guys to go outside and around to the back door." Off they went. Now Snubby and Pixie were alone.

Pixie was upset that Snubby blurted out the fact that she was abducted, saying, "I can't believe you just said that."

Snubby felt terrible that he betrayed his friend's trust and replied, "I'm sorry, Pixie, but you can't go on living this way. We care about you." Pixie nodded in agreement and waited for Snubby's next instructions.

"Okay, here's what we're going to do. Let's go up to the door and you call out to Scout. Make sure he is there; if he is, you know no one else is, and you feel safe with Scout, don't you?"

"Yes", she replied.

"Okay, call Scout."

Pixie shouted to Scout, "Are you there?"

"Yes, I'm here," he replied.

Snubby said, "Okay, Pixie, now you know it's safe to go out and I will hold the door open so you can come back inside if need be."

Pixie pushed her head through the door and reluctantly went through it; she called back to Snubby, "Everything is alright. Now you come out."

Snubby started through the door only to get part way. "Hey, fellows, I'm stuck."

"Oh, dear," Pixie said.

Scholar took charge, saying, "Scout, you get on one side and I'll get on the other. We'll grab onto his chain collar, and, Pixie, you say 'pull' when we are in place."

Pixie yelled, "Pull." They tugged with all their might and slowly but surely Snubby was pulled through the door.

Snubby was embarrassed, but managed to say, "See how easy that was, Pixie?"

Pixie took a deep breath of fresh air; she could smell the scent of spring in the air. Looking up at the sky, she thought the clouds were so beautiful.

Snubby shook the grass off of him, chuckling, "And now let's take a little walk."

Pixie ran toward the front door as she said, "What about our meeting? We need to go back inside now."

Scholar said, "Pixie, let's have our meeting outside today; it's such a beautiful day."

With enthusiasm, Scout said, "That's a great idea. Let's have it right here under this tree." Pixie walked very slowly toward the tree. Scout whispered, "Listen…hear the bird singing? That's a robin. Her babies hatched last week." Then he pointed up to the top of the tree. "You can see the nest right up there between those two big branches." Pixie looked up. "Did you see it?" Pixie nodded yes. "If you listen carefully, you will hear the babies tweeting when their mother returns with food and feeds them."

Scholar was wagging his tail with excitement. "This is a great place to have our meeting, and we can sit here and wait for the mother to return, so we can hear the babies tweeting."

Pixie looked up at the nest and asked, "Do you think we will be able to see the babies?"

Scout replied, "I'm not sure, but if we sit here long enough, we will soon find out." With that, Pixie sat down in the soft grass, continuing to look up at the nest.

Snubby ran home and quickly returned with an assortment of snacks. They had a picnic under the tree as they discussed the characteristics of the dogs they had researched. They were laughing and rolling around in the grass as they would take turns selecting a characteristic and then acting it out.

The most dramatic performance was put on by Snubby when he selected the characteristic "trustworthy." "Okay, you guys let me set the stage. I'm outside with the prez and he is chatting with a dignitary from another country. I hear them talking and I don't trust what that guy is telling the prez. So, what I'll do is spot a squirrel, chase it up a tree, and then run over to a different tree, look up at it, and start barking."

"I don't get it," said Scholar. "Well, then the prez will say, 'Stop barking…you're barking up the wrong tree.' And once he says those words, he will know that I was signaling to him not to trust the guy he's talking with! Genius, wouldn't you say?"

They had a glorious day; Pixie was much more at ease with being outside and even agreed to walk over to see their man cave the next morning. Also, they decided that there was no need for Snubby to continue working the graveyard shift since the majority of the data had been collected.

As soon as they left Pixie's, Snubby turned to Scout and said, "Please don't be upset with me. I know you have been wondering all day why I never told you before that Pixie was abducted."

Scholar spoke up, "He's not the only one who's wondering."

Scout was very hurt and angry; he had been hiding these emotions all day, not wanting to ruin Pixie's wonderful day outside. He lifted his head with a look of disappointment and said, "I'm sure you had a good reason, because you know how much I love Pixie."

Snubby told the story, almost crying as he spoke. "She didn't want me to tell you guys yet. She didn't intend to tell me; it just popped out when I confronted her about the take-charge attitude she has. She's afraid if she doesn't take control, something bad will happen to her again. So besides just getting her to go outside to see the cherry blossoms, maybe we can look for her family and someday get her home."

The three of them went silent, each taking a mental picture of Pixie, just in case she was not with them much longer.

With determination, and voice cracking, Scout said, "Maybe we can find something on the Internet."

Scholar, nodding his head in agreement, added, "Once I came across a website called Doggiefinders, or something like that."

They agreed not to mention anything to Pixie yet and pretend that neither Scout nor Scholar heard Snubby even mention the abduction.

In the morning, bright and early, the threesome walked over to meet Pixie and, to their surprise, she was sitting outside on the front step waiting for them.

Scout shouted to her, "I know what characteristic you are portraying: courage." Pixie stood up, wagging her tail, and ran over to meet them. Before taking her to see where they lived, Pixie wanted to sit under the tree with hopes that she could see the baby birds in their nest. All of a sudden they heard "tweet, tweet, tweet." Pixie looked up and could see the heads of three teeny, tiny birds. After that they headed down the trail to show Pixie their home.

Pixie loved their den; however, she had never seen so much stuff in her life: wooden crates, and old rugs spread out to serve as a carpet, with a large, heavy, plastic covering that kept most things dry if it rained.

Snubby disappeared and returned with a package. "This is for you, Pixie; it's from all of us." She was so surprised she didn't know what to say. "Open it," coaxed Scholar.

As she gently unwrapped the present, all of a sudden she saw this beautiful pink and white cloud of flowers. She could not contain herself and shouted, "It's a book with pictures of the cherry blossoms. I love it! I love it! I love it," at the same time jumping up and down.

Smiling, Scout said, "That's just the first part of your present. Tomorrow we're taking you to see the cherry blossoms in person."

Pixie stopped in her tracks; panicky, she said, "I couldn't possibly go; Mike will be here at one. I really appreciate it, I appreciate everything, but I can't."

"Now wait, Pixie," Snubby said reassuringly. "We have it all planned out. It will take us about one and a half hours to get there. If we leave at eighty-thirty in the morning, we should miss the majority of rush hour and arrive at the tidal basin about ten. We will hang out for an hour and be home by twelve-thirty." Pixie looked at her three friends and then glanced down at the beautiful book, nodding her head in agreement.

The next morning, the foursome began their journey; just as Snubby predicted, they arrived at 10:00 AM. Pixie could not believe her eyes; it was the most beautiful sight she had ever seen. "What a beautiful way to spend the first day of spring. I can see why you come here every year." Pixie gasped. She was overwhelmed by the beauty of the cherry blossoms; they looked like fluffy pink and white clouds, like the picture in her book. And whenever there was the slightest breeze, the petals would fall and looked like snowflakes falling to the ground. Pixie was running and jumping into these petals that now lay beneath the trees. Several times Scout looked around for Pixie and at first he didn't see her, since her snowy white fur blended in with the blossoms under the trees.

It was early; however, a lot of people were there: photographers with their tripods set up, and artists with easel and canvas, brush in hand, attempting to capture the beauty of the cherry blossoms. Scout figured they had been there for about an hour and he wanted to make sure Pixie got home before 1:00 PM. So he turned to Snubby and asked, "Is your stomach growling yet?"

"Yeah, it's growling. These blossoms make me hungry; they remind me of cotton candy."

"Then we better get going," Scout said. "I think it is getting close to eleven."

As they started their journey home, Pixie looked back at the blossoms cascading over the walkways and at the reflection of the blossoms in the water, from branches that were closest to the water's edge. As they walked home, they discussed how happy and lucky they were to have come that day; with rain predicted for the weekend, many of the flowers might have been gone by the next week.

CHAPTER 8

Pixie was enjoying her newfound freedom. As soon as Mike would leave for the day, she would open the door and run outside to take in the beautiful spring weather. Much of their research was complete; however, each of them had some loose ends to tie up, because the next meeting was to select who they thought were the ten most famous presidential dogs.

Some days Scout would take Pixie on long walks, giving Scholar and Snubby time to surf the Internet, looking for websites that had listings of lost or stolen pets. One day when walking with Pixie, he told her about his and Snubby's past life with the circus, and how they met Scholar. He was hoping that she would feel free to tell him about being abducted. After Scout's sad but sometimes funny circus stories, Pixie, snickering, said, "Now I know why you get so crazy whenever donkeys and elephants are mentioned."

Very matter-of-factly, Scout said, "Well, some canines say everything happens for a reason. Just think: if I hadn't left the circus, I never would have met you."

Pixie reached over and gave Scout a kiss then blushed. "Well, there is something I've been meaning to tell you" and she then proceeded with the story about her abduction that she had earlier told Snubby, explaining that she wouldn't have told him but he thought she was bossy. So she had to explain how bad things can happen if you don't have a plan and she couldn't afford to have Mike find out what they were doing and kick her out on the street. This time when she told the story, she didn't cry; she was thinking about what Scout had said — everything happens for a reason — and she was so happy they had met.

In the meantime, Scholar and Snubby had their work cut out for them; there were so many sites to look at, and they had only limited information about Pixie and her family. They knew she was abducted from the Washington, DC airport. But where was her family planning to move: Washington, DC, Virginia, or Maryland?

On Sunday, April 1, they met at their favorite meeting spot, under the big tree with the robins' nest. The babies were now about three weeks old, so in addition to them tweeting when their mother arrived with food, they were now old enough to begin learning to fly. Pixie was intrigued with the baby birds and sometimes worried what she should do if one of them accidentally fell out of the nest.

Scout told her, "If that happens, don't touch the baby bird; the mother will find the baby and take care of it." The meeting was ready to begin when Scout, being very serious, said, "Look, a baby fell out of the nest."

Pixie whimpered, saying, "Oh, no! Where?" At the same time, she quickly turned around, looking for the baby.

Scout then shouted, "April fools" and started laughing.

Pixie gave him one of her 'if looks could kill' stares and started chasing him around the tree. She caught up to him and pounced on top of his back, bringing him to the ground. "You want to laugh? I'll give you something to laugh about," she said as she pinned him down and started tickling him.

With authority, Scholar said, "Let's get our meeting underway."

Pixie told Scout, "Are you lucky!" then stopped tickling him and stood up. Scout was still rolling around in the grass, laughing and trying to regain his composure.

Everyone took their spots; Scholar asked, "Who wants to begin listing whom they selected as the top ten most famous presidential pooches?"

Looking at Scout, Snubby chuckled, "Maybe we should go round robin."

Pixie looked at Snubby, shaking her pom-pom at him in a threatening manner, and saying, "You're next."

Then all four of them started laughing. For the next two hours, they each presented their rankings and finally, after much haggling, determined that they could only agree on one dog.

Scholar said "Let's hear a drum roll, please..." Scout picked up a large stick in his mouth and started tapping it against the trunk of the tree. "And the presidential dog that came in first place, the one and only Bo Obama."

Over the next two weeks, Pixie spent most of her time outside with Scout since her students were now experts; sometimes she thought they even knew more than she did. When Pixie would try to encourage Snubby and Scholar to come outside with her and Scout, they would tell her that they had more research to do; of course they didn't tell her what kind of research.

They spent day after day searching for Pixie's human family. One day Snubby remembered something and told Scholar about Pixie telling him that her mommy loved her so much that she used to call her 'Lovie' and how she would watch television with her daddy, eating peanuts with him as he kept yelling, "Go, bears!" "She was so cute telling me that story; she said she didn't see any bears. I guess he was watching a football game. What do you think, Scholar?"

As Scholar started pounding away at the keyboard, he said, "I think we are on to something. Right here it says that the Chicago Bears went to the Super Bowl in 2007. That's around the same time Pixie would have been a pup...and guess what the head coach's name was?"

"What?" Snubby asked, getting so excited he started drooling on the keyboard as he got closer to see.

"Lovie Smith. I bet you her real name is Lovie. That's the name we need to look for when we try to find her family."

Pixie couldn't believe how quickly the last two weeks had passed by as she sat out front waiting for her friends to arrive. When they were in sight, she ran over to her favorite tree and plopped down. They said their hellos and Scholar kicked off the meeting. "Today we are going to talk about communication strategies; we have two types of communications, verbal and non-verbal." Looking at Snubby, Scholar said, "Why don't you begin by sharing what you have learned about non-verbal communication skills and give us a few examples?"

Snubby replied, "I would rather wait and talk about the verbal communication skills since that is my specialty."

Pixie smiled. "Yeah! He has his award-winning Barack bark; I would say it is definitely verbal."

Scout chimed in, "I would say it is definitely annoying. Then I'll start with the non-verbal communication skills; eye contact is the most important skill to remember." He looked over and winked at Pixie, then continued, "Seriously, it's important for you to look your owners directly in their eyes when they are talking to you. And sometimes you can gently rub against their leg or foot, but not when they have their good clothes on. Kisses are good, however, not too many and when they talk to you, sometimes do a cute little head tilt from side to side as though you understand every word they are saying."

Snubby warned, "But make sure you don't do that all the time or they will think something's wrong with you."

Scout concluded, "Those are the most important non-verbal communication skills that each of us needs to remember. Snubby, it's all yours."

Scout sat down and Snubby took the floor, boastfully stating, "When your master asks you to speak, sound one little woof; now, remember, only one little woof at a time. If you can learn to sound out a word, like I did with my Barack call, you also could possibly learn to sing along with your owner, as President Johnson did with his dog Yuki.

Finally, never cry wolf; what I mean by that is only bark if you have a reason, like to alert your owner that someone is at the door, that sort of thing." Snubby started walking back to his spot to sit down but stopped and asked, "Does anyone want to hear my Barack call?"

Cheerfully, Pixie said, "No, not right now" and added, "One more thing that is very important: always be engaging with children and guests." Everyone nodded in agreement and started discussing and practicing some of the basic tricks and commands they needed to excel in, such as sit, lie down, roll over, shake hands, and heel. They reminded Scholar that if he fetched the newspaper, he should return with it immediately, not stop off somewhere and read it.

They didn't schedule any future meetings; instead, they agreed to work during the week helping one another master these skills, so when opportunity came knocking, they would be ready.

CHAPTER 9

Snubby and Scholar told Scout they thought Pixie's real name was Lovie. He knew they were getting warmer and his heart sunk. He wanted the best for Pixie, thinking, *It's only a matter of time before Mike finds out about us.* Then he thought, *What will be will be. Everything happens for a reason. With all my heart I hope they find Pixie's family.*

It was a bright Sunday morning and Scout had taken Pixie over to the dump to pick up some cookies he had stashed. Snubby was searching the Internet and came across a website called Fidofinders. He clicked on 'Find Your Lost Dog' and typed in breed: poodle; color: white; size: small; gender: female; postal code: he wasn't sure what to put there. Snubby wondered where they moved to and what postal code they would have used: Chicago, Washington, DC, Maryland, or Virginia? Then he decided to start with Washington, DC and typed in postal code: 20007. He hit the enter key and a list with five names appeared.

He was so nervous he started perspiring, and kept look-ing over his shoulder to make sure Pixie wasn't coming through the door. Quickly, he scrolled down and there it was: the name Lovie. He clicked on it and all of a sudden a picture of Pixie popped up on the screen. His heart was pounding as he read, "Reward: five hundred dollars, abducted from the Washington, DC Airport on April 02, 2009." The phone number was listed for the owner, but no address. He quickly printed off the page, logged off the website, and ran outside to bury it.

Poor Snubby — this whole experience had overwhelmed him. He found a cool spot under their favorite tree to lie down and attempt to regain his composure. Pixie and Scout had stopped at the den, telling Scholar it was time for him to get up; they had brunch, and then the three of them headed back to Pixie's house.

When they arrived, they scampered over to Snubby. Pixie said, "We have a surprise for you," as she dropped the cookies in front of him.

He managed to wag his tail slightly, saying, "I'm not hungry right now." This was the first time they had ever heard him say he wasn't hungry, but since he looked okay and was not complaining, they let it pass.

They sat together enjoying their treat as they practiced the communication skills they were trying to master. Snubby was feeling more relaxed, so he joined in; he didn't want Pixie to think something was up.

It looked like it was going to rain so they said goodbye to Pixie and started back to their den. With a nervous tone in his voice, Snubby said, "Wait up. I have to get something." Puzzled, they watched him run over and start digging in the dirt, retrieving a piece of paper. Holding the paper in his mouth, he ran back to his friends.

"What's that?" Scholar asked.

"You'll have to be sitting down when I tell you. Let's get out of here," Snubby muttered as he ran toward home.

Scholar and Scout were baffled; as soon as they got home, Scout asked, "What's up, Snubby?"

He told them the whole story about the information he found on the website and then showed them the picture as he whined, "I know it's her. She has the same cute little nose."

The reality of losing Pixie had finally set in and Scout was speechless. Scholar leaned over. "Let me see what other information you have here. We have no address, only a phone number. We can't call them on the phone."

Scout took a deep gulp and said, "The White Pages has a reverse search capability; if you don't know the address, you can enter the phone number and it will give you the address and directions how to get there."

Scout was restless all night; he knew what he had to do but didn't know how to break the news to Pixie. The more he thought about it, he decided that he needed to be direct and not beat around the bush when he told her. The next morning before he left, he told Snubby and Scholar that he was going over to tell Pixie the news.

He picked up the picture of her and headed out on what would be one of the longest journeys of his life. As usual, Pixie was under the tree watching the birds when he walked up. He kissed her hello; she started talking about the baby birds again and wanted to know what happened when they left their nest. "Do they ever see their mother again?" she wondered.

Scout did everything he could to hold back the tears as he said, "I don't know, but I do know one thing: you're going to see your human mommy again."

At that, tears welled up in Pixie's eyes. "What do you mean see my mommy?"

Scout showed her the picture. "Your real name is Lovie; that's why she called you her Lovie." Pixie was visibly shaking as Scout went on to tell her how Snubby found the information yesterday and they thought it was important for her to know about this as soon as possible.

In a frightened voice, Pixie asked, "What should I do?"

Scout said, "It's up to you to decide what you want to do; however, I think you should be reunited with your family and I will do whatever it takes to make it happen. Stop crying, Pixie. I will come to visit you. You'll be so much better off there than living here. Let's go inside so we can look up the address and see where they live." Scout gave Pixie a kiss and she followed him inside.

She sat next to him as he logged on the computer and pulled up the White Pages. He entered the phone number, and their address with directions to their house was brought up on the screen. Scout was encouraged because it appeared that they lived in Georgetown. He did a quick Mapquest search, getting directions from the Fort Totten Transfer Station to that address. He exclaimed, "Look, Pixie, it's only six and a half miles from here. I can visit you every day."

Pixie halfway smiled, saying, "Let me think about it. I would love to be with Mommy, but I'm confused."

The next morning, bright and early, Pixie paid a surprise visit to her three friends. She told them that she had some good new and some bad news. With a somber expression, she began, "The bad news is that Uggie, the dog from the movie *The Artist*, went to the White House Correspondent Dinner over the weekend and I wasn't invited. And the good news is that my three best friends are going to take me back to my family." Everyone was relieved by Pixie's decision and impressed that, instead of having a doom-and-gloom attitude, she had chosen the high road. They decided that May 13 would be the day they would escort Pixie home. That was a Sunday, and it happened to be Mother's Day.

Pixie was worried about Mike; she didn't want him to come to work one day and she would just not be there. She felt it wouldn't be fair to him and he should have closure. So she asked Scout if it would be alright with him to sit under the tree with her and when Mike drove in, "we will jump up and run toward your den and then I will pause, turn around, run back toward him, stop, and make eye contact to tell him 'thank you,' then turn around and run back to you and then we will run off together."

Scout just shook his head at her in disbelief, thinking she had to be the sweetest doggie in the whole wide world. This meant that on Saturday, when Mike arrived at his usual time, Pixie would put on her show. And then she would hide out in the den until the next morning, when they departed to take her home.

Not only was Pixie worried about Mike, she was also concerned that her friends would not have a computer to use anymore. They assured her that their research was complete and they would make copies of the files they thought they might need.

On Saturday morning, as they planned, Pixie and Scout were sitting under the tree waiting for Mike to arrive. They heard the car drive up and he got out of the car to unlock the gate. They executed the plan just like they discussed and Mike just stood there with a dumbfounded expression on his face, thinking, *Well, I guess she found a new friend* and he wondered what that thing in her mouth was. It looked like a miniature statue of a dog.

When they arrived at camp, they found Snubby and Scholar sitting on pins and needles, hoping that everything was going as planned. They were relieved to see Pixie and Scout. All that day and into the evening, they reminisced and planned their trip for the next morning.

"Rise and shine," Scholar broadcasted.

Everyone had breakfast and headed on their journey; Scout led the group as they escorted Pixie to her new home. When they reached the corner of Potomac and Prospect Streets, Scout said, "You wait here. I'm going to walk Pixie to the door to make sure someone is home and that she gets in okay then I'll come back and meet up with you guys." Scholar and Snubby nodded in agreement. As they walked the two blocks, Pixie started crying. Scout said, "Don't cry, Pixie. You don't want your mommy seeing you this way. Remember I promised I will visit every day."

Sniffling, she said, "Okay, Scout."

Scout looked at the house number, verifying the address, and led Pixie up to the front door. In a calm voice, he said, "Now remember the plan. I'm going to hide right over there so I can see you and make sure you get in the house alright. Once I hide, you start your trademark yapping until someone comes to the door."

Pixie softly said, "Okay." Scout reached over and gave her a kiss as he slipped the Bo ornament into her mouth. He then got positioned in his hiding place and Pixie putting her ornament down, started yapping.

All of a sudden the door opened, and a lady looked down and said, "Lovie? My little Lovie, where have you been?" Lovie was squealing with joy as Mommy picked her up in her arms, carrying her into the house. In the doorway, the lady paused and quickly turned around, looking for a car or something that would indicate how Lovie had gotten there, but all she saw was a black and white dog running down the street and a tiny statue of a dog lying on the front porch.

They had a very quiet walk home; Scout hardly said a word, except to give directions. When they got home that afternoon, Scholar wanted to get their life back to normal as soon as possible because all they had been doing was moping around and worrying about Pixie for the past two weeks. He ran out to the dump and got Saturday's paper; when he returned, he said, "Listen to this: the president is hosting a really important meeting this coming weekend. It's called the G-8 Summit. Eight leaders from Britain, Canada, France, Germany, Italy, Japan, Russia, and, of course, the United States are meeting at Camp David, the presidential retreat."

"Where's Camp David?" Snubby asked.

"It's in Maryland, sixty-two miles from here," Scholar replied.

"I think we should go and meet these important people. You never know what kind of opportunities can pop up," Snubby said.

"Are you crazy, Snubby? It would take us a couple days to get there; the terrain is rugged in that area."

Snubby was excited and was crunching on a bone as he said, "Train! Great idea — we can take the train!"

Frustrated, Scholar said, "No, I didn't say 'train.' Stop crunching on that bone; you can hardly hear. I said 'terrain.'"

Dumbfounded, Snubby asked, "What does 'terrain' mean?"

"It means the surface features or general physical character of the land; that part of Maryland is wooded and happens to be very hilly."

Snubby picked his bone back up and started crunching it again, but paused briefly to say, "I was just looking out for you, Scholar, since you know how to speak German and French. Maybe you could be first dog in one of those countries."

CHAPTER 10

Every morning, as Scout had promised, he journeyed out to visit Lovie. It was about six and a half miles one way and it took him almost two hours to get there, but it was well worth the trip. Once there, they would talk and play in the backyard. Lovie's mommy was away volunteering at the White House kitchen garden. She would help pick the vegetables and talk with the children and volunteers about the importance of vegetables. She volunteered weekdays from 9:00 AM until 1:00 PM. This gave Scout and Lovie time to be together without Lovie's mommy seeing him.

On Saturdays and Sundays he would also sneak over to visit, but on a couple of these visits Lovie's mommy and daddy had seen him. One day when Scout visited, he found Lovie crying; she told him that she had heard Mommy and Daddy talking to each other about a stray dog they occasionally saw in the yard. They didn't like it and said that the next time they saw him they were going to call the Humane Society.

Scout's heart sunk as he managed to hold back his tears. Scout and Lovie decided that it was far too dangerous for him to visit in the daylight on Saturdays and Sundays, so they agreed he would visit after dark. Scout didn't mind these night-time visits because some days the temperature soared above one hundred degrees, breaking the all-time highs in Washington, DC.

For the next two weekends, Scout made the trip in the dark of the night to visit Lovie. Everything was going as planned until one rainy night as he was leaving Lovie's house, he stepped off the curb and while crossing the street, a car with no lights came around the corner and hit him. Scout flew through the air, landing about eight feet away on the sidewalk.

The driver stopped and quickly got out of his car, rushing over to Scout's side. He wasn't sure what to do; he didn't know if he should even touch this strange dog. But then Scout looked up at him with his big brown eyes and he managed to slightly wag his tail. The driver then ran back to his car, retrieved a large blanket, and wrapped it carefully around Scout. He then gently picked him up and placed him in the back seat of his car. Scout was confused and in terrible pain; he didn't understand why he could not move his back leg. During the ride, all he could think about was Lovie, wondering if he would ever see her again.

The car stopped in front of a large building and the man driving turned off the engine. Scout looked out the window, saw the sign on the building, and his worst fear had turned into a reality, for it read "District of Columbia Humane Society."

Snubby and Scholar were very concerned; it was time to bed down and their little friend was not yet home. The next morning they checked Scout's bed and found it empty; they were frantic! "Where could he be?" Snubby demanded.

Scholar cocked his head to the side and with a troubled look replied, "I don't know." For a minute they looked at each other with blank stares, not knowing what to do, then they decided that they should go to Lovie's house, and while on the way, try to retrace Scout's every step. It was Monday morning and they knew Lovie's mommy wouldn't be home, so they took off on their journey.

Along the way they didn't see any signs of Scout or anything that would give them a clue as to where he was. When they arrived, they found Lovie sunning herself on the porch. Upon seeing her two best friends, she quickly jumped up and ran over to them. She was so happy; her tail was wagging as she said, "Hi! I have missed you both so much. Thanks for coming to see me." She then gave each of them a big kiss. Snubby thought to himself, *Well, if Lovie is here, I can see that the two of them didn't elope.*

Scholar spoke up and said, "Lovie, it's great to see you, too. We really miss you, but we're here on official business. We are looking for Scout."

Lovie's eyes darted up and down as she insisted, "What do you mean you're looking for Scout? He's not with you?"

Snubby looked down at the ground; he couldn't bear to look into Lovie's sad eyes as he said; "Scout didn't come home last night."

Lovie panicked and began crying uncontrollably; she was barely able to squeak out, "It's all my fault. I shouldn't have let him visit me at night. How are we going to find him?"

Scholar leaned over and nudged Lovie with his nose as he said in a stern tone, "Lovie, get a hold of yourself. I have an idea. Do you remember when we did our research and came across the website for the DC Humane Society?"

Lovie sniffled and said, "Yes."

Scholar continued, "They had a profile for each of the pets that are in need of a home. If Scout was picked up by them, they will have information about him online."

Snubby chimed in, "Remember two weeks ago when your mom and dad said they would call the Humane Society? Maybe last night they saw Scout in the yard and when he left, they had him picked up."

Encouragingly, Scholar said, "So, our brilliant little Lovie—supervisor, trainer, computer technician—go find Scout for us."

Lovie perked up and asked, "What time is it?"

Looking down at his belly, Snubby said, "My stomach is growling. It must be about eleven."

Scholar shook his head in disbelief at Snubby's comment while telling Lovie, "You have plenty of time to log on to the computer. Run along now and take a look." Lovie ran up the steps and quickly scooted through her doggie door and into the house. Scholar thought to himself, *Thank goodness for computers and doggie doors.*

Within five minutes, Lovie returned, squealing with joy. "He's there! He's alive! He's there!"

They were relieved to know that Scout was in a safe place and being cared for. However, they were concerned if they would ever be reunited again. Snubby questioned, "Are you sure he's there?"

"Yes," she said. "I saw his picture; he looked so sad." Her eyes filled with tears.

Scholar placed his paw on Lovie's shoulder and said, "It will be okay, Lovie. Now tell us exactly what you read on the website."

Lovie paused, took a deep breath, and said, "Scout was in an accident; somebody hit him with their car."

Snubby looked up, tears welling in his eyes; he could barely manage to speak. "You mean my little buddy was hit by a car? Are you sure he is still alive?" He was shaking his head in disbelief.

Lovie sniffled and said, "Yes, he's alive; they keep status updates with new information on all of the pets. This way, people that are interested in adopting a specific pet will know when they can come in to visit and adopt their new pets. The latest information they posted about Scout said he was being cared for and is recovering."

This did not console Snubby in the least bit as his thinking quickly headed down the path of doom and gloom. Lovie reached over with her front leg and pressed her fuzzy pom-pom against his cheek to wipe away the tears. "Remember all of those late-night chats we had, discussing the power of positive thinking and how positive energy can make things better?" she asked.

"Yes, I do," he said as he looked up at her with bloodshot eyes.

Lovie gave Snubby a little kiss of confidence and whispered, "That's what the three of us have to do; we have to think positive."

Scholar nodded in agreement and asked, "Lovie, will you be able to check the website every few days and get a status on Scout?"

Lovie quickly responded, "Every few days? I'm going to check it every day." With that, Scholar and Snubby gave a little yip goodbye and told her that they would be back next week at the same time.

When Scout was taken into the Humane Society, the veterinarian gave him medicine that would make him drowsy, keeping him relaxed, while the doctor then proceeded to clean the wound and stitch up the cut on his leg. As Scout was waking, he heard a girl's gentle voice telling him how lucky he was that he wasn't hurt worse.

He kept very still as she softly ran her fingers through his silky hair. At first he did not know where he was or what happened to him; then all of a sudden it dawned on him — the Humane Society — and he tried to jump up. He yelped in pain then heard the gentle voice say, "Don't be frightened, little fellow. As soon as you're all better, we are going to find you a wonderful home. A lot of families would love to have a cute little dog like you."

Scout was taken aback by what she said and thought to himself, *Find me a home? I have a home.* He then closed his eyes as he thought about Lovie, Scholar, and Snubby, and how worried sick they must have been about him. With that, big tears rolled down his cheeks and then he drifted off to sleep.

The next day Scout had a much better outlook because he had figured out what he must do to get home. First, he was determined to get better as soon as possible so he could be adopted. After he was adopted, he would run away and join his friends at his real home: the Fort Totten Transfer Station. Life would return to normal and he could visit Lovie again.

Scout put his plan into action. First, he needed to exercise his leg so it would get better faster, and to do that he needed to get out of his cage. So every time the girl with the gentle voice would walk by, he would drag himself over to the door and look up at her with the most sincere and loving face he could muster, following her with his eyes as she passed by his cage.

His cute little antics worked like a charm; every day she would open his cage and let him out. At first he could only limp about, but soon he was able to scoot around and follow her as she went about her daily cleaning duties. So it would be easier for him to get out of his cage, she even changed his location from the third level down to the ground floor. At first Scout was concerned that being on the ground floor might make him less visible to families coming through to adopt. But he wasn't going to worry about that now; all he knew was that he was getting stronger and he would cross that bridge when he got to it.

All that week Lovie kept checking the website for updates. They had posted updates two times about Scout; the first said that he had an incision on his left hind leg and it was healing just fine, and the second one said he was getting stronger and in seven days he would be ready to be adopted by some lucky family. Lovie was relieved that Scout was not hurt worse by the car accident and he was getting better. However, the word "adoption" kept echoing in her mind; she was heartbroken by the thought of never seeing Scout again.

One day as she checked the updates, she saw a name on the website that she recognized: Doctor Oz. *That's the same name as the veterinarian Mommy took me to see when I came home.* She remembered his name because when she first met Doctor Oz, she thought about the cute dog Toto, who was the star in the *Wizard of Oz*. She carefully looked at a diagram that showed the layout of the Humane Society and saw that Doctor Oz's office was just down the hall from the dog adoption kennel. Lovie thought, *I'm not going to let Scout be adopted by some unknown family; it looks like Mommy and I are going to pay a visit to Doctor Oz.*

As promised, Monday morning Snubby and Scholar showed up at Lovie's. She told them that Scout was doing fine, and they were relieved. However, they were saddened by the fact that Friday's update on the website stated that Scout would be ready for adoption in seven days. Today was Monday and that meant he could possibly be adopted in four days; if that happened, they would probably never see him again.

Snubby, in a panicky voice, looked up at Lovie and said, "Will you help me think positive? I just can't figure out how this whole mess can have a happy ending."

"Guys, we know that having positive energy can make things better. Well, I need all of the positive energy you two can muster up because I have a plan. If it works, we will be seeing Scout before we know it."

Snubby was so excited he was drooling. "Will we see him next Monday when we visit?"

Lovie gave Snubby a big smile and winked. "Wish me luck. See you both on Monday."

Lovie's mommy was worried; all Lovie did for the last week was mope around. She would try to play with Lovie but the poodle was not interested and would just sit down and put her head on the floor. However, on Monday and Tuesday, she really got concerned when Lovie refused to eat her dinner. She even gave Lovie her favorite treats and Lovie turned her nose up at them. That's when Mommy decided that she should take her to see Doctor Oz for a checkup. She called and scheduled an appointment for Thursday.

Back at the Humane Society, Scout watched the smiles on families' faces as they came in and selected the dogs they wanted to adopt. They were so happy, hugging and loving their new family member. He remembered what Lovie had said about being first dog: you didn't have to be the president's dog; all it took was for your owner to love and believe in you, and in their eyes you were first dog. The more he thought about it, he knew he wouldn't have the heart to be adopted by a family that loved him and then run away, breaking their hearts. He was very confused, thinking he was in a no-win situation. He plopped his head on the floor and watched as more happy people came through the door and left with the new doggie loves of their lives.

On Thursday afternoon, Lovie's mommy came home and loaded her up in the car. Lovie was getting very nervous thinking about her plot, so much so that she was visibly shaking. Mommy said, "It's alright, honey, everything will be fine. We are just going to see Doctor Oz. You remember him, don't you?" All the way there Lovie had random 'what ifs' running through her head: *What if the door is not open? What if Scout is not there? What if someone already adopted him?* She finally told herself, *Stop!* And remembered what she had told Scholar and Snubby about needing all the positive energy they could muster up.

When they arrived, Mommy picked up Lovie in her arms and carried her into the building. Lovie was looking all around, trying to get her bearings straight; finally she saw a sign that had an arrow pointing to the dog adoption kennel. She was relieved; it was just as she had seen on the website and Doctor Oz's office was two doors down on the right. They walked into Doctor Oz's reception area and Lovie's mommy put her down on the floor.

Like a streak of lightning, Lovie took off running, bolting down the hall with her leash trailing behind. Mommy followed after her, yelling, "Stop, Lovie, stop!" Lovie was in luck; some people were opening the door to go in the adoption kennel, so she darted in between their feet and ran through the door. She cried out, "Scout, Scout, where are you?"

Scout could not believe his ears; he shouted, "Over here, Lovie, over here! Follow my voice." She followed his voice as she ran around the corner and there he was. They both started dancing around, crying with joy, as they pawed at the cage door.

Just as Lovie's mommy arrived and saw Lovie crying and pawing at Scout's cage, the girl with the gentle voice appeared. Looking at Lovie's mommy, she said, "It looks like these two know each other" as she let Scout out of his cage.

Scout and Lovie were putting on quite the show: kissing, squealing, running over and rubbing against Lovie's mommy's legs. She didn't know how Lovie knew this dog or why they apparently adored each other so much. She asked the girl who worked there what she knew about this little black and white dog. She pulled Scout's file and told her that he did not have any identification and was recovering from a cut on his left hind leg; he was hit by a car about two weeks ago on the corner of Prospect Street NW and Potomac Street NW. In shock, Lovie's mommy exclaimed, "That's just two blocks from my house."

She looked down at Scout and said, "Now that I think of it, you look like the little dog that ran away the day Lovie mysteriously appeared on my front door step on Mother's Day. I never put two and two together." She bent down, calling to Scout, "Come here, my little hero" as she gave him a big hug.

When she looked up, she saw Lovie inside of Scout's cage, gobbling up the food he had left in his dish. She smiled to herself and called to Lovie, saying, "I guess we can cancel our appointment with Doctor Oz. It looks like this is just what the doctor would have ordered." Lovie looked up, wagging her tail and smiling, and kept on eating. Shaking her head in disbelief, her owner said, "I have no idea on earth how all this happened and how Lovie was able to trick me into coming here. I guess it was meant to be."

The Humane Society worker smiled, saying, "Some things we'll never understand. But I agree, it was meant to be." They completed the necessary forms for Scout's adoption, and since no one knew his name, in the paperwork they named him Hero.

On the way home, Mommy kept telling them what smart little doggies they were. They sat in the backseat, grinning from ear to ear. That evening, Lovie explained the whole story to Scout about Doctor Oz and how she plotted to get Mommy to take her to see him. And she told him, "You may not be first dog, but now you're a Hero."

Scout snuggled up close to Lovie, telling her, "Just as you told us: it's not living in the White House that makes you first dog, it's being wanted and loved. Because of you I am now a first dog and you will always be my first lady."

CHAPTER 11

On Monday morning, Lovie looked up at the clock on the kitchen wall and said, "They should be here any minute." Scout couldn't wait to see Snubby and Scholar and tell them about his adoption. He wanted to surprise them, so he decided he would stay in the house until they arrived and then come outside.

Lovie was sitting in her usual spot on the porch when all of a sudden Snubby and Scout came running toward her. She stood up. "I have never seen you guys run like that before."

Snubby was out of breath but managed to say, "I can't wait to hear about Scout. How is my little buddy?"

Lovie said, "Why don't you ask him yourself?"

With that, Scout ran out the door. They were so happy to see each other, squealing, barking, and whining. Lovie was afraid the neighbors would call the police, so she had to tell them to quiet down. They sat together talking for hours as Lovie and Scout told them the whole story.

"So, should we call you Hero now?" asked Scholar.

"You can call me by both names, Hero Scout," he said laughing. "What have you two guys been up to?"

"We have been reading the newspaper every day to find out what big opportunities might be coming up so we can begin our networking."

Confused, Scout asked, "Networking?"

"Yeah, Scout, you have to have a social network in place so people will get to know you. Our plan is, when politicians and presidential hopefuls come to town, we can mosey on over and get acquainted."

Concerned, Lovie said, "Just be careful."

Scholar stood up and said, "Don't worry, we'll be careful. We love you both! It's getting late so we better take off."

As they headed down the sidewalk, Scout yelled, "So when are we going to see you guys again?"

Panting, Snubby replied, "The long walk in this heat is killing us. We'll make the journey again in a couple weeks."

Every day, Snubby and Scholar had the same routine. The first thing every morning, Scholar would run to the dump to get the newspaper; the news was a day late since he was retrieving newspapers that were in the trash to be recycled, but it didn't matter. The way he looked at it was old news is still news.

After searching the newspaper for social networking leads, they would spend the rest of the day practicing doggie etiquette. These were the rules of acceptable behavior they had researched and had practiced with Scout and Lovie. And in the evenings they rehearsed the verbal and non-verbal communication skills they wanted to specialize in; they wanted to stand out in the crowd and be noticed. And, of course, Snubby practiced his Barack greeting day in and day out.

One hot August morning, as usual, Scholar headed to the paper recycling area to pick up the newspaper. As he picked it up and read the headlines, he couldn't believe his eyes. Thinking, *This is the opportunity we have been waiting for*, he ran home as fast as he could. "Wake up! Wake up! Snubby, we've hit the jackpot."

Snubby lifted his head, rubbing his eyes with his paws. "What are you talking about?"

Scholar ran over and plopped down beside him. "Listen to this: the *Washington Post* headline reads, 'For the First Time in History, Three Months Prior to the Presidential Election, President Obama Invites All of the 2012 Presidential Candidate Hopefuls to a 'Let's Come Together' Dinner at the White House.'"

Snubby yawned. "So does that mean it will be a dinner for two, him and Mitt Romney?"

"No, it says 'all of the 2012 presidential candidate hopefuls', even those that dropped out of the race early. That means Michelle Bachmann, Ron Paul, Newt Gingrich, Herman Cain, and Rick Santorum, just to name a few. They are all invited."

Snubby sprung out of bed, saying, "Well, I guess all of our hard work is going to pay off. Do you have any more details?"

Scholar stopped to catch his breath and then continued, "Yes, yes, I'm so excited I feel like I'm going to have a heart attack! The dinner will be on Friday, September fourteenth. It will be held under a large tent that will be constructed on the South Lawn."

Snubby was pacing back and forth with excitement. "Outside! How perfect! Thank you, Athena!"

Scholar looked up, putting the newspaper down. "Who is Athena?"

Shocked by Scholar's question, Snubby replied, "You don't know who Athena is? She is the Goddess of Wisdom; dogs come to her for advice. I have been asking her every night, before I go to sleep, to help us. Scholar, I thought you knew everything. Didn't you study Greek mythology?"

Scholar picked the newspaper back up and said, "Well, whatever you're doing, Snubby, keep doing it. Let me see what other details they have...hmmmm, that's about it. Here's one more thing: the attire will be casual."

Quickly, Snubby reacted, "If mid-September temperatures are anything like this scorching summer we are having, I would think the dress code should be casual. Just imagine the guests dressed up in business suits, outside under a tent. They would have to call it the 'Let's Melt Together' dinner. And another thing that just came to mind, I hope the tent is not too close to those beehives the first lady put on the South Lawn for her organic honey." With an evil chuckle, he added, "On second thought, maybe that's why they're having the dinner on the South Lawn. As Scout would say, everybody knows that elephants and donkeys don't get along."

They looked at each other, thinking about Scout, wishing he were there to share in this news. In anticipation of the dinner, Scholar said, "We have four weeks to get prepared for our big début."

Soon enough, the big day was there. They spent all morning mapping out their plans, reviewing the exact route they would take to the White House and pin-pointing the location of the South Lawn. According to the map, it was located directly south of the mansion, and was bordered on the east by East Executive Drive and the Treasury Building and on the west by West Executive Drive and the Old Executive Office Building.

It would normally take them about one and a half hours to walk there, but today they wanted to take a leisurely stroll since they didn't want to be sweaty when they arrived. They were ready to head out. Snubby was struggling to get off the chain that was around his neck. "This dumb chain! I wish I could get it off; I look like a hoodlum."

Scholar was getting impatient. "That chain has been around your neck for I don't know how long. Fat chance you're going to get it off now. Let's go."

As they were getting ready to leave, Snubby picked up an old tennis ball that was lying there. They had only walked a couple blocks when Scholar glanced over and saw the ball in Snubby's mouth. "Get rid of that ball. You look ridiculous; you remind me of that silly Dubs I met one day when he was chasing his tennis ball all over Washington."

Snubby said, "I thought it made me look adorable."

"Snubby, I'm not trying to pick on you. But if you keep your mouth open holding that ball all the way to the White House; you will be a slobbery mess by the time we get there." Snubby stopped and dropped the ball. Shaking his head, Scholar said, "Look, you're already starting to drool. Go over there and wipe your mouth off on the grass."

Pouting, Snubby walked over to the grass and wiped his mouth off then thanked Scholar for telling him about the slobber.

When they arrived at the White House, they looked for all the landmarks they had discussed earlier that would help them find the South Lawn, and, sure enough, there was the big tent. It was now about 5:30 PM, and the staff was busy putting on the final touches. Snubby found a spot under the fence that he thought he could squeeze through and motioned to Scholar.

Once inside, they swiftly ran and hid in some shrubbery that was in the area, and then waited for the guests to arrive. The guests soon arrived, filing in one after the other. Small groups of people were standing together smiling, talking, and sipping beverages.

Scholar whispered, "There he is."

"Who? Where?" Snubby asked.

"It's the president with his beautiful wife and their two daughters."

Snubby was so excited, he was beside himself. "Look, look, who's the guy the prez just stopped to talk with? He looks just like me."

Scholar replied, "That's Newt Gingrich."

"Oh, yeah, now I remember…he's the guy who had the 'Pets with Newt 2012' website. So, when are we going to start mingling and meet these people?"

Scholar was getting nervous, not sure about how the whole meeting thing would play out, and replied, "After dinner is over would be my best guess."

Snubby thought, *That doesn't sound like Scholar; he is always very decisive. Hmmm…'my best guess.'* Snubby mulled this question over in his mind.

After everyone was seated for dinner, Scholar and Snubby decided to take a self-guided tour of the South Lawn. Snubby pointed. "Look over there. It's a huge swimming pool. That sure brings back bad memories. Let's walk over this way instead."

As they turned around and started walking in the opposite direction, Scholar commented, "I'm surprised we haven't seen Bo around somewhere."

Nonchalantly, Snubby replied, "I saw him; he's over there swimming in the pool."

Scholar cried out, "Swimming in the pool! Bo doesn't know how to swim!"

Off they ran as fast as they could. When they got closer, they could see that Bo was in the water and struggling. Scholar screamed, "We have to do something; it's our duty to save the first dog."

Snubby froze and stuttered, "Well...well, wait. Maybe the prez will see him."

"The president will see him? What are you talking about? The president is over there having dinner. We have to do something now!"

Snubby walked over to the edge of the pool, closed his eyes, and jumped into the water, with Scholar right next to him doing the same. Snubby swam over to Bo, got a hold of his collar with his teeth, and lifted his head out of the water. "Bo, I'm here to help you," he said then started propelling through the water like a little tug boat, pulling Bo toward safety.

Scholar was on the other side of Bo and was trying to convince him to let go of the ball he was holding in his mouth. "Bo, let go of the ball. Water is getting in your mouth. Let me hold it for you. I promise to give it back to you when we get out of the water." Finally, Bo released the ball; as promised, Scholar got the ball and held it in his mouth as he swam alongside Bo.

Snubby was getting out of breath. "We're almost there. Keep your mouth closed and move your legs like I am. It's the doggie paddle." Then Snubby started bellowing, "Bar-r-r-rack! Bar-r-r-rack! Bar-r-r-rack!"

The first family and their guests looked around at each other, wondering where that unusual sound was coming from. Sasha exclaimed, "Daddy, it almost sounds like your name. Let me see where it is coming from." She ran toward the pool and then started screaming, "Daddy, Daddy, come quick! Bo is in the pool."

The president quickly jumped up from the table and made a mad dash toward the pool, with some of his guests following. When he approached the pool, he couldn't believe his eyes. Snubby and Scholar were at the shallow end, pulling Bo out of the water. The president rushed over to Bo's side and knelt down beside him to make sure he was alright. Then he looked over at Snubby and Scholar and asked Bo, "Who are your friends? Don't worry; I don't know their names, either, so let's call them top dogs."

Bo stood up, shook some of the water off of him, ran over, and kissed Malia and Sasha; he was so relieved to be out of the pool he was running around in circles chasing his tail. And then he darted out of sight, leaving his ball behind. By this time, Snubby and Scholar had an audience, since many of the guests had gathered around the pool, listening to the story about the rescue and how these two top dogs, as the president called them, saved Bo's life.

All of a sudden Bo ran back, holding a tomato in his mouth; he ran up to Snubby and dropped it in front of him. Scholar, who was still holding Bo's ball for safe keeping, dropped the ball in front of Bo so he could pick it up; however, Bo rolled the ball back to Scholar with his nose. Laughing, the president said, "Well, it looks like Bo has a present for each of you. I can't believe he is parting with his favorite food and his favorite toy. He must also think you're top dogs."

Snubby and Scholar were exhausted from the rescue and sat down; even though stunned by all of the people and the flashing of cameras, they just sat there without moving a muscle. Two staff members came with towels and started drying them off and the first lady directed the staff members to take the top dogs to a ground-floor room in the West Wing. The guests and the first family then returned to finish their dinner.

Snubby and Scout could not believe their eyes when they entered the room; it was beautifully furnished, with French doors leading out to a patio. The staff person told them that this was where they would be staying and to wait there until they returned with water and food. Snubby looked at his tomato and Scholar looked at his ball as they thought this wasn't exactly what they imagined social networking would be like.

The big buzz that evening was about the two strays that rescued Bo. At the end of the evening, the president announced that Sunday, September 23, was 'Dogs in Politics Day,' also known as 'Checkers Day,' and in recognition of that day, an event was planned in the afternoon at the White House. He invited everyone to bring their families and join in the festivities, adding, "If you are dog parents, by all means bring your dogs."

He added that during the celebration, he would be honoring the two heroes they witnessed pulling Bo out of the swimming pool that evening, and said that they would be staying at the White House until he could find a home for them. He left his guests with the following thought: "Please consider adopting one or both of these remarkable animals."

When Newt was saying his goodbyes, he asked the president, "What breed of dog is the one Bo gave the tomato to?"

The president eagerly replied, "I believe he's an English bull dog. Why, are you interested in adopting him?"

Being non-committal, Newt said, "I was just wondering. His face looks so familiar."

The president approached Mitt as he was leaving. "Hey, Mitt, since you declared September as 'Responsible Dog Owner's' month when you were governor of Massachusetts in 2006, I hope to see you at our event on 'Dogs in Politics Day.' In the meantime, think about adopting one or both of these top dogs."

Smiling, Mitt said, "Thanks for the great evening" and he shook the president's hand as he departed.

Snubby and Scholar had finished their dinner and were outside sitting on the Oval Office patio, eavesdropping. Very proudly, Snubby asked, "Did you hear Newt asking the prez about me?"

Scholar looked sad. "Yes, I did hear him. That's great, Snubby. Did you hear anyone ask about me?"

Snubby didn't know what to say since the answer was no, but he replied, "I'm not sure. The noise was so loud with everyone talking."

They walked back into their room, snuggling deep into a large feather pillow bed that had been brought for them to sleep on.

"Snubby, with all of this excitement, I haven't had a chance to tell you how proud I am of you. You were so courageous, jumping into the water like you did, putting your fears aside to save Bo." Snubby didn't reply. Scholar looked over and his friend was sound asleep.

Later on the evening news, there was a breaking story. "Good evening, this is Jim Vance with News Four, bringing you the nation's capital eleven o'clock nightly news. To start your weekend, I have a heartwarming story to share with you. This evening at President Obama's 'Let's Come Together' dinner, he had an unusual event happen and it has nothing to do with politics; it has to do with courage. Take a look at this. Here is a picture of the top dogs, as the president refers to them. They rescued Bo, the first family's pet, from the swimming pool this evening..."

Lovie was lying on the floor in front of the television and glanced up at the screen when she heard Jim Vance say "top dogs." She couldn't believe her eyes: a picture of Scholar and Snubby was on the television. Nudging Scout, she said, "Quick! Look! Wake up!"

Scout yawned as he opened his eyes and looked up at the television screen. "Oh! Wow! They did it, they did it, they got to the White House and met the president...and look at all the other important people they got to meet." He jumped to his feet. Lovie and Scout were both standing at attention with their eyes glued to the television screen, listening to Jim Vance.

"On Sunday, September twenty-third, the first family will host an event celebrating 'Dogs in Politics Day' and a special awards ceremony will be held honoring the president's top dogs."

Scout and Lovie's mommy was watching the two of them; she was amused at how excited they got when they saw these dogs on television. She shook her head as she said, "Come on, you two, it's time for bed. You'll get to see those pooches in person at the awards ceremony on Sunday. Mrs. Obama has invited all of the kitchen garden volunteers to attend."

Scout and Lovie stopped dead in their tracks and then with excitement started running around in circles, chasing their tails. As she watched them, she thought, *I don't get it; sometimes it seems as though they understand every word I say.*

The next morning, bright and early, the president and Bo visited Snubby and Scholar at their quarters in the West Wing. The President told Snubby and Scholar all about the plans for September 23, and that they would be staying at the White House until he could find good homes for them. He talked to them just as he would talk to a human; little did he know they understood every word he was saying.

As he got ready to leave, he stopped, looked back, and said, "I'll be on the campaign trail all week, so take care of Bo for me." Scholar and Snubby ran over and gave the president a kiss goodbye. Smiling, the president looked at Snubby and said, "Let me hear your unusual bark again."

Holding his chest out proudly, Snubby called out, "Bar-r-r-rack." As he left the room, the president shook his head, laughing and thinking to himself, *That does sound like my name.*

Bo stayed behind to visit with his two heroes, wagging his tail and looking at them with admiration. As they stood there looking at Bo, it occurred to them that they had never heard Bo talk. They knew that he heard and understood them because he followed the instructions they gave him when they were in the pool.

Snubby finally blurted out, "Bo, can you talk?"

At first Bo just looked at them, then he slowly looked all around, making sure no one was there, and finally said, "Yes, I can talk, but when Senator Kennedy had me groomed by his obedience trainer for this important position, they taught me everything I should do and not do, and I didn't think I was supposed to talk."

Scholar walked over and fondly looked Bo in the eyes, saying, "You can talk to us. We can only hear each other, and humans can't hear us."

Tucking his head down, Bo asked, "How did you know I didn't know how to swim?"

Trying to build Bo's confidence, Scholar answered, "We read about it. You're very important and were voted the most famous first dog."

Bo whimpered, "Everybody knows everything about me. Do you know how embarrassing it is to be a water dog and not know how to swim! They even printed that humiliating fact on my baseball card."

Snubby leaned over, nudged Bo, and began his pep talk. "Bo, we have eight days before the big shindig. I can teach you to swim! And then when the prez gets back, we can surprise him, plus I don't think we would be able to save you again; you weighed a ton with all that wet hair on you." That made Bo laugh and he was looking forward to his swimming lessons.

Snubby and Scholar were curious about all the different people they saw walking around the West Wing. Bo told them that this was where the presidential staff worked, and he described the layout, telling them about the cafeteria, gym, and pool.

Snubby thought, *A pool…this might be the perfect place to begin Bo's swimming lessons. Start out small and work our way up.* "Hey, Bo, let's take a walk so you can show us the pool."

As they walked down the hall, all of the staff members were fussing over them and commenting that those were the two dogs that saved Bo. Snubby and Scholar loved it, but it just added to Bo's embarrassment.

When they got to the pool, Snubby shouted, "Perfect! Bo, this is where we will begin your swimming lessons. We'll meet you here tonight when everyone goes home."

Reluctantly, Bo said, "Tonight, why tonight?"

Trying to comfort Bo, Scholar said, "Don't be frightened; you already know we can save you if anything goes wrong, which it won't."

Bo shook his head in agreement. At that, Snubby explained his plan to Bo. "We will meet every night for your lessons; we'll begin our lessons in the West Wing pool and work our way up to the big outdoor pool. Just think how surprised your family will be when they see that you learned to swim."

Snubby and Scholar couldn't believe how fast the next seven days flew by. Their days were filled with the White House staff members showering them with attention and the appointments they had with Bo's personal groomer, who cut off that ugly chain around Snubby's neck; he was so relieved. The groomer told him that the president was going to get him a new collar.

They didn't know whether they were coming or going, but loved every minute of it. One day Malia and Sasha even took them on a tour of the White House. As they walked down the halls and into the various rooms, they recalled all of the interesting things they had read about the first dogs that had lived there. After that, they visited the first family's second-floor residential quarters, where Bo was eagerly awaiting their arrival.

It was in the evening before the big day and they had just finished up Bo's last swimming lesson at the big outdoor pool. Bo was swimming like a pro, and they could hardly wait for the family to see him in action. That night, Scholar looked up at Snubby and said, "Look back, what has been the most important lesson we have learned along our journey to be first dog?"

Snubby reflected back and said "Lovie told us, you don't have to live in the White House to be a first dog. There are a lot of people who have dogs, and those people think their dogs are first dogs." They nodded in agreement and then drifted off to sleep.

Bo knew that the president liked to swim in the mornings, and since he was scheduled to come home Saturday night, Bo figured at the usual time, which was 9:00; the president would take a dip in the pool. And normally on weekends the entire family would go to the pool with him, so he asked Snubby and Scholar to meet him there at nine.

That morning when the family was getting ready to go to the pool, Bo kept circling them, wagging his tail; he wanted to make sure that they didn't forget to take him with them. The first lady asked, "Bo, what are you so excited about?"

When they arrived, Snubby and Scholar were lying on the pool deck, sunning themselves. The family was happy to see them and was walking over to greet them, when they heard a big splash. Everyone quickly turned to look and, to their amazement, Bo was swimming across the pool. When he got to the other end, he walked up the stairs and ran over to the family.

They were so proud of him; they even told Bo that they were going to update his baseball card, stating that he now knew how to swim. The president looked up at the two top dogs and thought to himself, *I wonder if they had anything to do with this.*

That morning, Lovie and Scout's mommy and daddy were getting them ready for their special visit to the White House. Lovie and Scout were so excited; they had been counting the days, and today was finally here. As Daddy drove, they sat in the backseat. Lovie leaned over and told Scout, "Wait until they see us; they'll be so surprised."

Scout replied, "We'll find out soon because we are almost there."

"How do you know that?" Lovie asked.

In a nostalgic tone, he replied, "This is the route I mapped out for them if, for some reason, something would have happened to me and I was not here to lead them. You remember how bad they were with directions, don't you?"

Lovie cuddled close to Scout, resting her chin on the back of his neck. Before they entered the gate, a security officer came to the window; he recognized Mommy and waved for them to enter. Lovie and Scout had the backseat windows all smudged up with wet prints from their noses. When they got out of the car, they kept searching and searching for their friends.

Mommy had stopped to talk with someone, and then all of a sudden, Snubby and Scholar raced over and abruptly stopped just before almost running into them. At first Mommy pulled back on the leash, but then as she watched the four of them dancing about and crying with joy, she dropped the leash. She thought, *Here we go again...another 'believe it or not' event that will go unexplained.*

Stuttering with excitement, Snubby asked, "How...how did you find us?"

Lovie shrieked with excitement, "We saw you on TV! It was fantastic!"

"Our eyes almost popped out," Scout cried.

Scholar told them the whole story of what happened that evening when they rescued Bo and described the royal treatment they had received for the past week.

Snubby inquired, "Do you get to use the computer much these days?"

Lovie whispered, "No, not really. We are worried that Mommy might find out, and she thinks we're weird enough already."

They all laughed, then they heard the president announce, "May I have my top dogs, front and center?"

Lovie reached over and kissed Scholar and Snubby as she told them, "That's for good luck."

Snubby and Scholar ran over to the platform where the president was standing and sat next to him at the podium. The president thanked everyone for coming to celebrate 'Dogs in Politics Day' and then added, "We have another reason to be here; it is to honor these two courageous fellows that are sitting beside me."

He briefly told the story of Bo's rescue and then turned to Snubby and Scholar and said, "And it is my privilege to introduce to you the top dogs." Everyone started applauding; the president then continued, "I don't know their real names because they are strays, but my family and I were blessed the night they decided to pay us a visit and rescue Bo. However, I hope before this day ends, they will be given names and adopted by a loving family. Let's turn this amazing act of courage into an act of kindness."

The first family then presented Snubby and Scholar with beautiful gold collars; both were engraved with the words "Top Dog." The president looked down at Snubby and Scholar and said, "Come over here, you guys, there are a couple of people I would like for you to meet."

With their tails wagging and walking right in step with him, they followed. The president was delighted that Newt and Mitt had decided to attend the event. He walked over to where they were sitting, shook their hands, and said, "I would like to personally introduce you to my two heroes."

Newt and Mitt knelt down and gently patted them on their heads and rubbed their backs. The president asked them if they had thought anymore about possibly adopting one of them. Newt replied, "Well, my wife and I have discussed having a dog," as he reached down and started petting Snubby again.

The whole time Scholar was staring into Mitt's eyes, saying to himself over and over, *Eye contact, eye contact*, while using his little puppy dog look, with an occasional cocking of his head from side to the side.

Newt continued, "He sure is a cute little fellow, but I can't imagine having a dog that every time he barks, I hear your name." He looked over at the president and chuckled.

Snubby looked up at Newt, his tail wagging, and gave a loud, clear, "Woof!" Everyone started laughing. Scholar looked at his friend, thinking, *Way to go, Snubby.*

Mitt bent down and was looking into Scholar's eyes as he remarked, "He looks so intelligent."

Scholar immediately held out his right paw for Mitt to shake. Puzzled, Mitt asked, "Look at that. Why is he holding his leg out like that?"

Barack grinned and replied, "He wants to shake hands with you."

Mitt gave Scholar a big smile of approval, reached out for his paw, and gave it a warm shake. Scholar thought, *This man has a very kind face and you can always trust someone who has a firm handshake.*

Snubby's "woof" and Scholar's handshake sealed the deal. Newt decided to adopt Snubby and Mitt adopted Scholar. The best news was that Mitt and Newt decided that since Snubby and Scholar were best friends, they could have play dates, and Barack added that sometimes they could visit Bo at the White House.

Lovie and Scout were listening to the discussion, and with tears of joy streaming down their faces, they walked up to Snubby and Scholar. Lovie said, "We are proud of you, and so happy about your new homes. You're not only top dogs now you're first dogs too."

With sad eyes, Scout said, "Well, I guess this means we won't be seeing you anymore."

Snubby replied, "At least you two have each other and Scholar and I will be able to see each other on play dates."

Scout dropped his head. "That's all good, but it won't be the same. We'll miss you."

Scholar looked at them and winked, saying, "No worries. I have some very intelligent friends that have proven, time and time again, where there's a will, there's a way."

CPSIA information can be obtained at www.ICGtesting.com
Printed in the USA
LVOW080231121112

306876LV00004B/47/P

9 781478 151920